D0001632

Phyllis Reynolds Naylor

ONE OF THE THIRD GRADE THONKERS

illustrations by
Walter Gaffney-Kessell

A Yearling Book

With special thanks to Edwin and Darlene Bull,
Jim Hinton, Sr., Jim Hinton, Jr., and also to Captain
Jim Seabrooke of the Coast Guard, for their time
and assistance.

Published by
Bantam Doubleday Dell Books for Young Readers
a division of
Bantam Doubleday Dell Publishing Group, Inc.
1540 Broadway
New York, New York 10036

ISBN: 0-440-40407-X

Reprinted by arrangement with Macmillan Publishing Company, on behalf of Atheneum

Printed in the United States of America

February 1991

10 9

OPM

To
the towboat men
of Joliet, Illinois

CONTENTS

1

THE THIRD THING

Three things happened to Jimmy Novak when he was in the third grade.

His mother had a baby, which wasn't bad, because every time people brought Benjamin a present, they brought a little something for Jimmy as well.

Next, Jimmy hurt his knee and had an operation, which wasn't the best thing in the world to have happen, but it wasn't the worst, either.

And finally, a cousin came to visit who was the last person in the world Jimmy wanted to see. But that didn't happen until later.

It was after the operation that Jimmy first heard the word *Thonker*. Dr. Sheen, the surgeon, was a little bit nuts.

"Hi, Thonker, how you doing this morning?" he

said each time he came into Jimmy's room. And after Jimmy left the hospital and went to Dr. Sheen's office for visits, the doctor would say, "Just climb up on the table, Thonker, and let me look at that knee."

On one of Jimmy's visits to the doctor, he saw his friend from school, Sam Angelino, and realized that Dr. Sheen called all his patients "Thonkers," which showed just how crazy he really was.

"See you in three weeks, Thonker," he said as Jimmy started out the door, and then, to Sam, who had broken his arm on the slide, "Come on in here, Thonker, and let's see how you're doing."

Jimmy and Sam grinned at each other. The next day at school they called themselves "Dr. Bonkers' Thonkers," and the name stuck.

It wasn't a club at first. It was only Jimmy and Sam walking around the playground, with the other boys tagging behind. Jimmy was on crutches and Sam had his arm in a cast, and every day at recess, the other boys begged to try out the crutches or to write their names on Sam's cast. They wanted to know what an operation was like and whether Jimmy had felt any pain when he was asleep. Jimmy said maybe he did feel a little something when the doctor started cutting, even though the last thing he remembered was his dad giving him the thumbs-up sign in the hallway.

The other boys talked, too, about how Sam had fallen backward down the steps of the slide and hadn't cried, even though they could see the bump on his arm where the bone had broken. It was understood that if you were going to be a Thonker, you ought to be a little braver than the other children; something had to have happened that you wouldn't want to go through again in a million years.

So when Peter Nilsson came to school one morning with the story of how the brakes had failed on his mother's car at the drawbridge—the car with him and his mother in it—and how the car had almost, but not quite, gone in the canal, Peter became one of the Thonkers, too. Even the teacher had heard about the accident on the evening news.

From then on it was just the three of them—Jimmy, Sam, and Peter—but there wasn't another boy in the whole third grade who didn't wish that he, too, was a Thonker.

They had special T-shirts, for one thing. In Jimmy's, Sam's, and Peter's families, however, you didn't just walk up to your mom and say, "I want a T-shirt with *Thonker* on the front." You said, "What can I do to earn some money for a T-shirt?" Jimmy had to hose out the garbage cans and paint them; Peter had to scrub the front porch and wash some windows; and Sam had to baby-sit his little sister and change her diaper twice. But the next day, all three boys came to school in new black T-shirts with the word *Thonker* on the front, in big red letters dripping blood, and on the back of each T-shirt it said, *Do or Die*.

They always rode their bikes in formation, too. Sam decided that they ought to rank themselves according to how long each of them had had to be brave.

Jimmy, it was decided, was Number One, because it took a lot longer to get well after a knee operation than it did after a broken arm. They argued about who would be Number Two, because almost going off the end of the bridge into the canal was scary as anything for Peter, but since the fear only lasted a minute, it was decided that Sam with his broken arm would be Thonker Number Two. So whenever they rode around Garnsey Park or over to Holy Cross School, Jimmy, who was the largest, went first; Sam, who was shortest and heaviest, came next; and Peter, who was tall, brought up the rear.

By the time March came around, Jimmy decided that third grade wasn't so bad. He had a new baby brother, lots of new gifts, and he himself was Thonker Number One.

And then, the third thing happened: The cousin came.

The week had started out well, actually. The wind felt warmer, and the Thonkers were already talking about what they were going to do over spring vacation. The Novaks' house was on a street at the very top of a steep hill. The hill was so steep that the Novaks' backyard sloped all the way down to the alley. The garage, in fact, was built under the end of the backyard, like a cave.

Jimmy's dad said he was tired of driving his car all the way around to the alley, and that, if Jimmy liked, the Thonkers could use the garage for a club-house—till next winter, anyway. Jimmy was in heaven.

It was *then* that the third thing happened, the worst thing, the cousin from Cincinnati. Mother got a call from her sister, Lois, who was going to have a heart operation. Lois wanted to send seven-year-old David to stay with the Novaks until she recovered. He would be flying up the week before spring vacation.

Jimmy walked slowly out the door and down the backyard. He climbed over the fence at the bottom, dropped to the alley, and opened the door to the clubhouse.

It was cool inside the garage, with only the light from the door coming in. Jimmy sat down heavily in one of the chairs and stared at the words Sam had painted on the wall: "The Thonkers: Rough, Tough, and Terrible."

A year ago, when Jimmy had last seen his cousin, David cried when he hurt his mouth eating a Frito; he got scared in a movie and Aunt Lois had to take him home; he carried around a large teddy bear with one leg missing; and he still wet the bed. And now, that very same cousin was coming here.

2

GETTING READY FOR
WEIRDO

On Saturday, Jimmy sat at the kitchen table with his parents, watching his mother feed Benjamin strained beets and spinach. Little globs of red and green trickled down the baby's chin. When he sneezed, he looked like a Christmas tree. Jimmy got a cloth and helped mop up.

"I'm going back to work this evening, Jimmy," his father told him, taking a last bite of mashed potato. "Bet you're going to have yourself a time over spring vacation."

Sure, Jimmy thought. *With Weirdo David coming for a visit.* "Vacation's still a week off," he said aloud.

Jimmy's father, Bart Novak, was first mate on a towboat, the *Herman C.* The towboat pushed barges down the shipping canal from Chicago to Joliet, on

6

down the Des Plaines River to the Illinois River, which led at last to the Mississippi. At New Orleans, it turned around and came back up river again. When he was on the job, Bart Novak ate his meals on the towboat, and slept there, too. He would work thirty days at a time and then have thirty days off to spend at home with the family.

"David will be here when you get back," Mother reminded him.

"That's right. When's the little fellow coming?"

"Tomorrow. We'll drive to the airport to meet him."

"Well, tell him I've got a big old hug waiting for him when I get home," said Father.

"Better not squeeze him too tight; he'll wet his pants," Jimmy said.

"Jimmy!" Mother scolded.

George and Marsha Evans, friends of Mom and Dad's, came by to pick up Jimmy's father. George had started work on the towboat a few months ago as an engineer, and the two men worked the same thirty days.

Jimmy sat out on the steps, watching his dad leave. When Bart Novak went out to the car with his duffel bag over his shoulder and a suitcase in one hand, he looked like a sailor going to sea, Jimmy thought. Father had big, broad shoulders and a thick back, and Jimmy wanted to look exactly like him when he grew up; work the barges, too. He could sign on to work for a summer when he was seventeen, Dad had said, as an engineer's helper. He'd keep the inside of the boat clean, make up the bunks, maybe even splice some line.

By the time the Evanses' car was out of sight, Jimmy knew what would happen next: Mother came out of the house with Benjamin and handed Jimmy his jacket.

"Let's go get some ice cream," she said.

Whenever Father went to work on the towboat, Jimmy's mother took him and the baby up the street for an ice-cream cone, just to make herself feel better. Benjamin, of course, always made a mess with his, but Mother didn't mind. What bothered her was going back to an empty house.

"Well," she said at the ice-cream parlor, "at least this time we'll have David with us. The house won't seem so empty."

Jimmy turned his fudge ripple cone around and around in his hand, licking the sides. He would have to be very careful of what he was about to say, he knew, but there was still a chance he could keep David from coming.

"Why can't he stay with a neighbor?" he asked politely.

"Lois thought of that, but you know how David wets the bed sometimes. Lois was afraid the neighbors might not understand—might tease him."

Jimmy tried again. "Why doesn't David's grandmother come and take care of him, then?"

"Because both of his grandmothers are dead," Mother told him. "Grandma Slater was David's grandmother too, you know."

8

"Well, why couldn't Aunt Lois put an ad in the paper and hire some nice woman to stay in the house and look after David there?"

"Because Lois doesn't want to leave him with someone he doesn't know. It's going to be hard enough as it is."

Jimmy squeezed his cone too tightly and ice cream dripped out the end. He decided to try one last time. "Well, if *you* were going to the hospital for a heart operation and my father and grandmothers were dead, I wouldn't want to go stay in another city; I'd want to be there with you," he said.

Mother smiled at him. "That's very sweet," she said, and Jimmy smiled back. He was beginning to feel a bit more hopeful. He imagined his mother calling Aunt Lois when they got home and saying, "Lois, maybe we're making a mistake. I think David should stay right there in Cincinnati near you."

Mother bent down and wiped Benjamin's face with a Kleenex. "But staying in Cincinnati won't work," she said. "Number one, David's too young to be able to visit his mother in the hospital, so it wouldn't do any good to keep him there. Number two, Lois wants him here . . . ," she picked up her bag and slung the strap over her shoulder, ". . . so that if anything happen to her, David can live with us."

For a moment Jimmy couldn't swallow. Could hardly breathe, even. It was too horrible for words. And then, when he thought that nothing in all the world could possibly be worse than having David live

9

with them, Mother said, "Just so David won't feel so lonely, Jimmy, he's going to sleep in your room on the trundle bed."

Jimmy stared at the remains of the sugar cone there in his hand. Slowly he got up from his chair, walked to the trash bin, and dropped the cone inside.

Benjamin cooed all the way home, but Jimmy didn't say a word. He couldn't. All his words seemed stuck in his throat. The Novaks' house wasn't very big, and there were only two bedrooms, but somehow he had thought that his cousin would sleep on the couch. The trundle bed under Jimmy's own bed was supposed to be for *friends* when they spent the night—Sam Angelino or Peter Nilsson. Never in his life did Jimmy think that David would come all the way from Cincinnati to sleep in his room. *Forever,* maybe.

When they got home, Jimmy went straight to his room. He put away all the things he didn't want his seven-year-old cousin to touch: his transistor radio, his quartz watch, his Legos, his airplane, and his Matchbox car collection.

Then he dug around through some old posters in the back of his closet until he found the ones he wanted. He took down a picture of a fighter plane above his bookcase and put up a poster for *Alien* instead. He took down a picture of the world's longest roller coaster and put up a poster of zombies in its place. Maybe David wouldn't sleep in his room after all. Maybe he'd *beg* to sleep on the couch.

After he had gone to bed that night, however,

Jimmy thought about how it wasn't exactly David's fault that he was coming; it wasn't as though he *wanted* to, anymore than Jimmy wanted him there. He went to sleep hoping that Aunt Lois might get well faster than the doctors expected and that David would go home within a week. *Anything* was possible.

3

WEIRDO

Jimmy sat in the back seat of the car on the way to the airport. He always sat in back with Benjamin, because it was his job to keep the baby happy when they drove anywhere.

Benjamin was strapped in his car seat, making sleepy little singsong noises and blowing bubbles of spit at the same time. Benjamin's face was as round as a bowl and his hair was short and dark, like Dad's. Jimmy, though, had light brown hair like his mother's, and they both wore it long; Mother's was down to her shoulders, and Jimmy wore his over his eyes.

Every so often Benjamin would start to fuss, and then Jimmy would pick up his fuzzy dog and make little yipping noises as he pressed it against Benjamin's stomach. Or he would dangle the house keys in front of Benjamin and shake them up and down.

"Almost there," said Mother, turning in at the airport.

Jimmy told himself that David might have changed a lot in the past year. Maybe by now he had gained ten pounds. Maybe he was taking karate lessons. "Killer," Jimmy used to call David, sort of as a joke. Maybe now the nickname fit.

"You never know," said Mother as they stood at Gate 12 and waited for the plane from Cincinnati.

It was Jimmy who saw him first; he couldn't believe that it was David. His cousin seemed to have shrunk instead of grown. He looked at least ten pounds lighter. As David came up the hallway, the flight bag slipped farther and farther down his arm, until finally David just grabbed hold of the strap and dragged it along the floor.

"Oh, David!" said Mother, reaching down and giving him a hug.

"Hi, Aunt Carol. Hi, Jimmy," David said.

"Hi, Killer. How you doing?" Jimmy asked.

David smiled a little and handed the flight bag to him. "It's so *heavy!*" he said, as they moved on to the baggage pickup. "Mother sent almost all my clothes. You'd think I was going to be here forever!"

Jimmy's heart sank.

There were two large suitcases on the baggage ramp. Mother got a skycap to carry them outside, and finally everyone was back in the car. David sat up front.

13

Jimmy felt too numb to even think. David didn't walk, he shuffled; he didn't sit, he slouched; he didn't talk, he whined. Jimmy, Number One of the Third Grade Thonkers, would have this second grade wimp in his bedroom for nobody-knew-how-long.

"Do we get to drive by the prison?" David asked as the car headed home.

"Why, certainly, David, if you like," Mother said.

Jimmy closed his eyes. Every time David came to Joliet, he wanted to drive by the prison. Aunt Lois said it was so he could see for himself how big and strong it was, and that the bad men were locked up tight.

The first thing anyone ever thought about when they came to Joliet was Stateville, the prison. Joliet had lots of parks and a beautiful theater with mirrors on the walls, but all people thought of when they heard the name Joliet was the prison. They didn't even say Joliet right; they said "*Jolly*-et" instead of "*Joe*-lee-et."

All the way there, David chattered on about the awful things that had been happening to him lately. A bee got in his bedroom and almost stung him; a dog almost knocked him down; he hurt his hand on the swings and got a stomach ache that lasted a week.

"Gracious!" said Mother. "We're going to take very good care of you while you're here, David."

"Excuse me while I throw up," Jimmy whispered under his breath. He began to wish he had covered the walls in his room entirely with scary posters and wondered if he could find even more in his closet when they got home.

Jimmy always knew they were near the prison when signs appeared along the side of the road that said "Do not pick up hitchhikers." Square white signs with black letters. This time David noticed them, too.

"Is that because the hitchhikers could be escaped convicts?" he asked, wide-eyed.

"You got it," said Jimmy.

"I heard about a man once that picked up a hitch-hiker and after they got out of town the hitchhiker shot him and cut his body up in pieces and put the parts in different boxes and mailed them all over the country," said David.

Mother stared at him. "That's a *horrible* story, David!" she said.

"I know," David told her. "I had to sleep in Mother's room for two whole nights after I heard it because I was so scared."

Oh, brother! Jimmy said to himself.

"Well, we won't be picking up any hitchhikers," Mother promised.

"There it is!" David exclaimed finally as the large, low prison came into view, set far back from the high-way and surrounded by a thick concrete wall. "Do you think I could ever see inside there, Aunt Carol?"

Mother suddenly veered to the right, slowed the car down, and turned in the long driveway. "You know what?" she said, "I'm going to find out right now. I'm going to ask if they have tours."

Jimmy flattened himself against the back of the seat in embarrassment. He couldn't stand it. He knew that Mother was going out of her way to be kind to David because of Aunt Lois, but this was too much. Half the people in Joliet didn't even know where Stateville was, had never driven by it, and didn't care. And here was this seven-year-old weirdo from Cincinnati who wanted a tour!

They had to park the car in the visitors' section, near a high barbed-wire fence surrounding a lawn, and walk over to a guardhouse. Up in the towers along the wall, prison guards with guns looked down at them. Jimmy swallowed. The guardhouse was locked, and when Mother rang a bell, a man inside pressed a buzzer, which allowed the door to be opened. David was wide-eyed with wonder.

"Ma'am?" said the guard behind the desk when Mother stepped inside with Jimmy, David, and Benjamin. Jimmy was just sure that the guard thought they had all come to visit their father.

"Excuse me," said Mother, "but I have two young boys here who would like very much to see inside the prison. I wonder if it's possible."

Jimmy felt his face redden. How *could* she?

"I'm sorry," said the guard. "No one under eighteen. That's the rule."

"Oh, what a shame," said Mother. "This young fellow right here is from Cincinnati, and he's been wanting to see inside Stateville for years."

The guard just smiled. "Let's hope he never does,"

he said. "Have a good day, now."

They walked back to the car again with guards looking down and the man in the guardhouse staring after them.

Jimmy could hardly speak he was so angry. As he put Benjamin back in his car seat he said, "Why did you *say* that, Mom? *I* didn't want to see inside Stateville."

"I'm sorry," said Mother. "I just figured that *two* boys wanting to see the prison might get us somewhere. I didn't mean to embarrass you."

That evening, the only thing that David liked on his plate was applesauce.

"I don't like meat loaf," he said, pushing his to one side. "I *never* eat carrots, and I can't *stand* scalloped potatoes!"

For the first time, Jimmy thought he saw a trace of impatience on his mother's face.

"Well, David," she said brightly, "I guess you'll just have to fill up on bread and applesauce, then, because that's all we're having for dinner."

"No dessert?" asked David.

"Not unless you eat your meat loaf," said Mother.

David didn't eat his meat loaf so there wasn't any dessert—for *anyone*.

"Put your dishes in the sink," Jimmy snapped as David started to leave the table.

"Why?" David asked.

Jimmy was about to say *because I said so* when Mother answered for him. "This is a boatman's family,

18

David, and when men are working on a boat, they always carry their dishes from the table to the sink."

"Oh," said David. He put his fork on his plate beside the untouched meat loaf and carried it over to the counter.

Mother tried to hide a smile. "Bart always says that they thank the cook, too. It's sort of a boatman's tradition."

"Even if they didn't like the food?" David asked.

"Well, they usually do," Mother explained.

David looked back at the table. "The applesauce was good," he said.

"Thank you," said Mother.

While Mother did the dishes afterward, Jimmy took Benjamin into Mother's bedroom to change his smelly diaper. There was only one thing to do, he decided, as he cleaned the baby's bottom and dusted it with talcum powder—make David so uncomfortable here that he'd beg to go back home and live with a neighbor.

Jimmy put a fresh diaper on Benjamin, put the baby in his crib, then carried the dirty diaper through the living room, right in front of the chair where David was watching television, right in front of David's nose, in fact, then circled on back to the bathroom.

4

PILLOW TALK

Jimmy got in the bathtub first that night so that David wouldn't take all the hot water. As he was washing his feet, however, he thought of all the things David might be getting into back in his room, so he hopped out, pulled on his pajama bottoms, and went down the hall.

"That's my bed," he said, when he found David sitting on it, holding his teddy bear.

David looked down at the trundle bed. "That one's too low," he complained.

"Too bad, kiddo," Jimmy said, and hung up his clothes.

"There are all kinds of things that go crawling around the floor," David protested.

"Only Benjamin," Jimmy said.

David sighed. He went down the hall to the bathroom. Jimmy pulled out the posters in his closet and looked through them again. This time he found one of a great white shark with its mouth open. The shark had about a million teeth and seemed to be coming right at you. Jimmy taped it to the wall at one end of the trundle bed, where it would be the first thing David saw in the morning when he woke up, the last thing he saw before he went to sleep. Then Jimmy climbed in his own bed and lay there waiting for David.

He wished he had bought a black-light poster instead. If this was a black-light poster, he could turn out all the other lights and the shark's teeth would glow green.

He could hear water gurgling down the drain in the bathroom, and a few minutes later David came into the room, wearing his Bambi pajamas, his blond hair still wet, a pajama leg sticking to one moist knee.

He stopped dead still, his mouth open.

Jimmy closed his eyes and tried not to laugh. He heard the floor squeak. He heard footsteps in the narrow space between his own bed and the trundle bed. When he opened his eyes at last, he saw David standing on one end of the trundle bed, leaning forward with his head against the poster, right at the opening of the shark's mouth.

Jimmy sat up. "What the heck are you doing?" he asked.

"Measuring," said David. He put one finger on the wall at the top of his head, another against the wall

near his chin, then stood back. "I don't fit," he said, looking relieved.

"Ha!" said Jimmy. "You don't have to fit. Sharks never swallow you whole. They just take big bites."

David dived down into the trundle bed, pulling the teddy bear with him and the covers up over his head. Jimmy reached over and turned out the light.

He heard David's blankets rustle.

"Don't you leave a night light on when you sleep?" came David's voice.

"Nope."

"Don't you even leave your door open, just a little?" the voice said, beginning to squeak.

"Nope."

The room was quiet for a few minutes.

"I feel snakes," David said suddenly.

Jimmy rolled over. "Go to sleep, David."

"I feel *snakes!*" David said again. "They're under the sheets."

"They're only lumps in the mattress," Jimmy told him.

"Which would you rather be?" asked David. "Eaten by snakes or swallowed by a shark?"

"I'd rather be asleep," Jimmy said.

The room got very, very quiet this time, and after a while Jimmy thought that perhaps David had gone to sleep at last. He was just starting to drift off himself when he heard his cousin say, "I heard of a boy who found a shark in the toilet."

"That's crazy," said Jimmy.

"No, it's not. He lived near a river and a shark swam in out of the ocean and up the river and got in the boy's swimming pool and had babies and one of the babies went in through the pipes and came up in the toilet."

"That's the dumbest thing I ever heard," said Jimmy.

"Good night," said David.

Jimmy lay there with his eyes wide open. He wondered if maybe that *could* happen. The Novaks' house wasn't far from the canal. The canal was connected to the Des Plaines River, the Des Plaines to the Illinois, the Illinois River flowed into the Mississippi, the Mississippi into the Gulf of Mexico, and the gulf led to the sea. It could happen.

Mother came to the door of the bedroom. "You boys in bed already?" she said. "David, I thought you might like to call your mother—just to let her know that you got here okay and to tell her good night."

David got out of bed and went to the phone in the kitchen. Jimmy heard his mother dial the long-distance number, then David's voice, telling Aunt Lois about the plane trip, the prison, and the shark in Jimmy's room.

When David came back to bed, he said, "I wonder what would happen if a shark ever lost his teeth. Then he wouldn't be able to eat anybody, would he?"

Jimmy sighed. "I suppose not."

"Do you ever worry about losing *your* teeth?"

"No, David. I never worry about that at all."

"I do, sometimes," said David. "I worry about a lot of things. Like getting a job."

"Getting a *job,* for Pete's sake?"

"I mean, how can I look for a job if I don't have a car, and how can I buy a car if I don't have a job?"

"David, you are really wacko, you know? You ever hear of a bus?"

"Hey, that's right! I could always take a bus, couldn't I?" David said. The minutes ticked by and the bedroom grew quiet. "How would I know which bus?" he asked.

"David, will you please go to sleep?" said Jimmy. "You're driving me nuts."

"Sorry," said David, and turned over.

Jimmy didn't know what happened next because he finally started to dream. But sometime in the middle of the night, when he got up to go to the bathroom, he opened his bedroom door and it sounded as though he had opened a cupboard full of pots and pans.

Jimmy turned on the hall light just as Mother came hurrying out of her bedroom in her robe.

There, tied onto the knob of Jimmy's door with shoelaces, was a brush, a flashlight, a spoon, and one of Jimmy's Matchbox cars that he hadn't hidden away.

"What on earth?" said Mother, and she and Jimmy stared at David.

David rose up sleepily on one elbow. "It was so if

any convicts escaped in the night and tried to get in this room, we'd hear them," he said.

Jimmy went on into the bathroom and closed the door behind him. That settled it. David would have to go.

5

DAVID MEETS
THE THONKERS

On Monday, Sam Angelino and Peter Nilsson stopped by for Jimmy on their way to school. The Third Grade Thonkers always walked together. Jimmy went outside where Sam was waiting in his brown leather jacket. Peter Nilsson was wearing a sweat shirt with a picture of a giant fist on the back. Jimmy himself was wearing his football jersey with the padded shoulders. Then David came out wearing a wool sweater with red and green reindeer on it and carrying his "Little House on the Prairie" lunch bucket.

"Who's *that*?" Sam whispered.

"This is my cousin, David. He's staying with us for a while," Jimmy told them.

"Hi," said David, and as the three Thonkers started off, he tagged along behind.

Jimmy had promised his mother that he would show David to the second grade classroom, where he would be going to school until Aunt Lois was better.

"This is David," Jimmy said to the second grade teacher. All the other children in the room were staring.

"We're glad to have you, David," said the teacher. "Jimmy's mother told me you'd be staying with us a while. Just put your lunch bucket back there with the others, and we'll find a place for you to sit."

"See you," said Jimmy, and went on down the hall.

"How long is he going to be here?" Peter asked Jimmy as they took their seats in Miss Verona's classroom.

"Till his mother's better; she's having an operation," Jimmy said.

"I can't believe he's *your* cousin!" Sam told him. "He looks like he belongs in nursery school."

"He's not going to be hanging around with *us,* is he?" Peter asked. "He's not going to be one of the Thonkers?"

"No way," said Jimmy.

All morning long Jimmy hoped that David would make new friends in second grade and have someone else to talk to. But when noon came and the first, second, and third graders gathered in the all-purpose room for lunch, David brought his "Little House on the Prairie" lunch bucket right over to the table where the Thonkers were sitting, opened it up, and made a face at everything Jimmy's mother had packed for him.

"I don't like salami, I don't like oranges, and I

don't like oatmeal cookies," he whined. "Doesn't anyone have a Twinkie?"

"Eat it," said Jimmy, frowning.

"I'll trade mine for yours," David said to Sam. "What kind of sandwich do you have?"

"Chicken gizzards," said Sam, hiding a smile.

David stared. He turned to Peter. "What's yours?"

Peter pretended to peek between his two slices of bread. "Liver and horseradish," he said.

David's mouth twitched. He glumly pulled all the crusts off his salami sandwich and took a tiny bite.

When afternoon recess came around, Jimmy and Sam and Peter started a game of kickball in one corner of the field. David tried to join in, but the first time the ball hit his leg, David limped over to the fence, rubbing his shin.

Well, he'll just have to find some friends his own age to play with, Jimmy thought later as he copied his spelling words from the blackboard. Letting David sleep in his room and walk to school beside him every day was enough. Jimmy certainly didn't have to play with him all the time.

During the last hour of the day, as the students were turning in their history papers, Jimmy stapled them together for Miss Verona and got a staple in his thumb by accident.

"Ouch!" he said softly.

"Wow!" said Peter, staring at the staple stuck partway in Jimmy's thumb. "Bionic man! Let me try that!"

He took the stapler, gave it a press, and the staple

must have gone in a little deeper because Peter sucked in his breath. But when Sam tried it, he didn't make any noise at all, and there they were—the three Thonkers with staples stuck halfway into their thumbs.

When the bell rang, they went outside to wait for David, trying not to laugh.

Peter took a stick of gum from his jeans. "Want some gum?" he asked Jimmy's cousin.

"I only eat Juicy Fruit," said David.

"You're in luck," said Peter, holding it out. As David took it, his eyes fell on the staple. He gave a little scream and backed away.

"What's that stuck in your thumb?" he squealed. "Pull it out!"

Peter pretended to notice it for the first time. "Oh, yeah," he said. "I guess it's a staple."

"Well, what do you know?" said Sam. "I've got one, too!"

"So do I!" said Jimmy.

"H—how did they get there?" David asked.

"Well, we're a club, see," Sam told him. "The Thonkers. You hang around with us, you've got to get staples in your thumbs and everything."

With that, the three Thonkers sauntered on home, David trailing behind, holding his "Little House on the Prairie" lunch bucket in one hand, his Flintstones pencil box in the other, wearing his bright wool sweater with the red and green reindeer on the front, and looking worried.

6

MAKING PLANS

Jimmy could tell right away that Mother was going to keep them busy while David was there—so busy, she hoped, that David couldn't worry too much about Aunt Lois and her heart operation.

"I got tickets for us to the magic show at the Rialto next week," she said as the three of them, and Benjamin, sat at the table after school drinking Hi-C punch. "And one of these days we're going to the Brandon Road lock and wave at Dad. He called this morning, Jimmy, from Lemont, and said they've been waiting for more barges. He thinks they'll be coming back through Joliet on Wednesday."

It didn't keep David from worrying, however. "How's my mom?" he said in answer.

Mrs. Novak reached over and wiped a dribble of

Hi-C from Benjamin's face. "When I called at two, she was still in surgery. I'll try again at five. Heart operations take a long time, you know."

David didn't say anything more. He went into the living room and turned on the TV.

Jimmy put his glass in the sink. "The guys are coming over in a little while," he said. "I'll be out in the garage, Mom. Okay?"

Mother only nodded.

Jimmy waited. And because she didn't say what he thought she was going to say next, he said it himself. "I don't have to take David with me everywhere I go, do I?"

"It's up to you, Jimmy," was what Mother said.

"I mean, Sam and Peter and I are a club," Jimmy added.

"I know," said Mother.

When Jimmy saw his friends coming, he went out to meet them. David stayed in the house.

"You mean David's not going to tag along?" Peter asked.

"He's busy watching cartoons," Jimmy said.

"Donald Duck, I'll bet," said Sam, and Peter laughed. Jimmy almost wished he hadn't said anything about cartoons. He really didn't know what David was watching.

The day was sunny, and their clubhouse in the garage was a little warmer than usual.

"Man, this is going to be a great place this summer,"

said Sam. "We can eat and sleep out here and everything."

"It might even be warm enough to sleep out here over spring vacation," said Jimmy. "I'll do almost anything to get out of the house while David's there."

They sat around an old cable spool that they used for a table, something that had once been on a barge. Jimmy had brought out a bag of pretzels and the boys took turns thrusting their hands in the cellophane package, making plans for camping out in the garage.

They talked about school and they talked about David, but it wasn't long before they were talking about the one thing they talked about most—the scariest thing of all—the thing that some of the boys who lived near the canal often talked of doing but seldom did: riding the railroad bridge. That would be even better than staples in their thumbs.

"This time," said Jimmy, "we're really going to do it."

Sam and Peter stopped chewing.

"When?" Peter asked.

"The last Saturday of spring vacation," Jimmy told them. "After we've been sleeping out here all week. Then, when we sneak down to the canal, no one will miss us."

"Sure. We can do it," said Sam.

"Easy," said Peter.

No one spoke again for a while. It was the first time Jimmy had ever said those words aloud—about really sneaking off. He had often wondered what it would be like if he did ride the railroad bridge. The drawbridges in Joliet opened at the center when a tall boat went through, each half of the bridge swinging upward. But the railroad bridge did not divide in two. It was built high over the canal so that boats could pass beneath it, and was only lowered when a train needed to go across. Afterward it rose again like an elevator, and went forty feet up in the air, where it stayed until another train came by.

The trick was to run out on the bridge some evening at dusk, just after a train had gone over it, and see how high up you had the nerve to ride before you jumped off onto the bank. Without the bridge tender catching you, too. Jimmy had imagined again and again how he would walk into school some morning and tell the other boys about riding the bridge. That was the most awesome thing he could think of.

"We've got to plan this carefully," Sam said. "What are you going to do about your cousin? If David finds out, he'll tell."

"He won't find out," Jimmy said, "because he's not going to hang around with us."

It was as though speaking of David brought him there. The boys heard footsteps on the gravel outside and then a tiny knock on the garage door.

"Jimmy?" came David's voice.

"Speak of the baby and here he is," whispered Jimmy. "Who's there?" he yelled, knowing all the while.

34

"David," came the voice.

"Say the password," called Sam.

Jimmy and Peter stared at Sam.

"What password?" whispered Jimmy.

Sam just laughed. "I don't know, but whatever he says, it'll be wrong."

"I don't know the password," called David.

"Sorry, then. You can't come in," Sam told him.

There was a pause. "Jimmy, your mom says that dinner's ready," David said.

"Okay, he heard you," Peter called.

"Jimmy, you'd better come!" David said, louder. "She says the hamburgers will get cold."

"Scram!" yelled Sam.

The footsteps went away.

When his friends went home and Jimmy went back up to the house for dinner, he noticed the silence at the table. Benjamin was slobbering over a cracker that he held in one fist and looked as though he were trying to stick it up his nose. But no one seemed to be talking.

Jimmy thought maybe it was because he had been too slow coming to dinner. But then, when Mother put the salad on the table, she said, "Well, Aunt Lois is in the recovery room now, so at least we know the operation's over."

Jimmy knew then that it wasn't quiet he was feeling there in the kitchen; it was worry.

"How is she?" he asked.

"They didn't really tell me anything. The nurse

just said that Lois was in the recovery room, and that I could talk with the doctor tomorrow. No news is good news, I guess."

Jimmy looked over at David, who was carefully arranging pickles on top of his hamburger. David said nothing at all.

That night, after the lights were out, however, David asked, "What's a recovery room?"

"A place you go after an operation until they're sure you're okay," Jimmy told him. He remembered that from his leg operation.

"How long does that take? Before she's okay?"

"It all depends," Jimmy said, not knowing what else to tell him. Then he added, "But hundreds of people have heart operations every day, David, and they turn out just fine." He wasn't even sure if that was true, but it sounded good.

David fell asleep fairly soon; Jimmy could tell by his breathing. But it was a while before he felt sleepy himself. It wasn't Aunt Lois that Jimmy was thinking about, though; it was the railroad bridge. Now that he had actually said they were going to do it, there was no turning back. Thonkers never turned back.

He imagined him and Sam and Peter quietly creeping out of the garage and heading down to the canal on that particular Saturday about dusk. They could usually count on a freight train using the railroad bridge near McDonough Street on Saturday evenings.

He imagined them making their way through the weeds and bushes to the water's edge, waiting while a towboat or two came down the canal pushing a long line of barges ahead of it, a red light on the port side of the lead barge, a green light on starboard, and a flashing yellow light between them. The boys would wait in the bushes until the bridge came down. The metal would creak and groan as the bridge began to lower until it was even with the tracks on either side. After a while they would see the light of a train coming far down the tracks from Rockdale. The moment it had passed, the boys would dash out on the bridge and ride it up. Just thinking about it, Jimmy's heart raced. He wondered how long he would wait before he jumped.

And then, just before he went to sleep, Jimmy thought of the stories he had heard his father tell his mother—stories Jimmy wasn't supposed to hear. About the bodies the boatmen found in rivers sometimes—people who had fallen in drunk, or those who jumped on purpose. Towboats had to make time, Jimmy's father said, and they weren't supposed to stop, not even for a body, unless it was "a little bitty baby."

What boatmen were supposed to do was to tie up the body to the nearest tree and radio the local police so they could come for it.

As Jimmy lay there in bed, he wondered if boatmen would ever stop the boat for the body of a boy—say, an eight-year-old who had climbed out on a railroad bridge some night, lost his footing, maybe, and fallen in.

7

CATCHING DAD

The towboat, the *Herman C.*, had finally got its barges together and was coming back through Joliet on its way to New Orleans.

If the weather was good, Jimmy's mother always took Benjamin and him down to the canal to wave to Dad, and sometimes, at the Brandon Road lock, if the line of barges was so long that only half of them could get through at a time, the captain might let Jimmy's dad get off the boat for a while to visit with the family before the *Herman C.* hooked up its tow again and moved on.

Jimmy and David had scarcely gotten in the door after school on Wednesday before Mother said, "I called Lockport lock and the *Herman C.* just went through. Let's go see Dad at Brandon lock and then we'll stop at McDonald's."

There was a mad scramble to get everyone in the car with seat belts buckled. Mother quickly started the engine. Once they were on Broadway, Jimmy had a clear view of the canal at every intersection. The Jackson Street bridge was just going down, so the *Herman C.* must have already gone through. Seven blocks farther on, the Jefferson Street bridge was just starting to go up. They were gaining on the boat. Jimmy knew they would make it.

David was very confused about locks. "Why do there have to be gates?" he asked. "Why can't boats just go straight through to the ocean?"

"Because the water would flow much too fast, David, and there would be too many shallow places," Mother told him. "Big boats can't use our canal unless it's deep all the way along. That's what the locks do— hold the water back and make it deep."

Dummy, thought Jimmy, even though he remembered asking the very same question once himself.

"You mean first they pour the water in one part of the canal and the boat goes through the gates and then they pour it in another part?" David asked.

"That's right," Mother said. Jimmy realized that she hadn't said one word yet about Aunt Lois.

At the Brandon Road lock, the three-decker *Herman C.,* with its pilothouse making up the third story, was just moving up to the lock gate when Jimmy and David ran up the steep sidewalk to the fenced area at the top. Mother came hurrying behind them, pushing Benjamin in his stroller. Even before Jimmy reached the fence, he could hear the one long and one short blast of the *Herman C.*'s horn.

The gray and white towboat itself was at the very back of the line-up, pushing its eight barges on ahead. The two at the very front, side by side, were empties, Jimmy could tell, because they rode high on the water, but the other barges rode so low that only a foot or so rose above the surface. These were carrying oil, Jimmy guessed.

On this side of the lock gate, where Jimmy stood, the water was so low that he couldn't even see it at the bottom—only the gray concrete wall of the lock streaked with stains. A steady stream of water was gushing through an opening in the gate, but Jimmy knew it would take a while for the water in the lock to reach the level where the towboat waited.

Boatmen were moving about on the first barge, getting their ropes—lines, as they called them—ready. George Evans was probably somewhere on board, but Jimmy couldn't see him. Dad, though, was right out there in front. He was in charge of all the deckhands, and was showing one of the new men how to lasso a timberhead to hold the barge fast. The deckhand tried to do it, but the loop missed. When Jimmy's father swung the line, however, the rope slipped easily over the thick metal post on the dock. Jimmy smiled.

After that Bart Novak taught the man where to place the rope bumpers to protect the barge as it went through the narrow lock. Each bumper was fastened to the end of a long rope, and Jimmy saw his dad dip the bumper in the water first. He knew why. Sometimes, if a bumper was dry, it caught fire from the friction of all the scraping.

"Looks like I got company!" Jimmy's dad called out when he saw his family lined up along the fence. He tipped up the bill of his cap and grinned broadly. All the men wore billed caps, which kept the sun out of their eyes during the day, and shaded them from the arc lights at night.

Mother picked up Benjamin and pointed his face toward Dad, but Benjamin was looking at a pigeon that had settled on a timberhead farther on.

"Can you get off for a little while?" Mother called.

"If Henderson's in a good mood," Dad yelled back, and Jimmy knew he was talking about the captain. "I'll see."

The part Jimmy liked best about coming to the lock was that no matter how big the other men looked there on the barges, his father always looked bigger. Not fat. Big. Arms as thick as cantaloupes. Thighs as big as watermelons. Bart Novak could sit down at a table and eat everything on it, Mother always said, and ten minutes later he'd be hungry again because he did as much work as ten men put together.

Dad always joked about work, though—always pretended he never did anything. All the boatmen talked like that. "I'm not afraid of work," Dad would say. "I'll sit down right next to it!" And then he'd laugh.

Jimmy could see his father go back into the pilothouse and talk with the captain. The captain smiled and nodded, and then, in one leap, Bart Novak in his fire-engine red life jacket hopped from the barge onto the wall of the lock, followed the sidewalk down to where his family was waiting, and came striding through the gate of the visitor's area.

"Hey, *David!*" he yelped, swooping down on Jimmy's cousin and tossing him over one shoulder, then whooshing him down to the ground again. He swooped down on Benjamin too, there in Mother's arms, rubbing his grizzled cheek against Benjamin's, making him squeal. He kissed Mother and then he grabbed Jimmy and gave him a hug.

"How's Lois?" he asked Mother.

"She's still in intensive care, but the nurse said that this was usual after a heart operation."

There was something about Mother's voice—or perhaps it was the look in her eyes as she said it— that made Jimmy know she was worried. He stole a look at David, but David was pushing a stone with the toe of his sneaker, driving it along a crack in the sidewalk and over toward the water's edge. It was as though he wasn't even listening.

"We've got some greenhorns working the tow this trip," Dad said. "Don't know an eye wire from their elbows. I've got to get back on when we start through the lock." He took Benjamin from Mother and they all walked along the sidewalk on the visitors' side of the fence as the water in the lock rose higher and higher.

"Darnedest thing happened on our way up to Lemont," Father said, and Jimmy smiled. Every time his father worked on the boat, he came home with a new story. Mother said he must make half of them up, but Jimmy was sure he didn't.

"What happened?" Jimmy asked, hoping the story would be a good one, with David there to hear it. A dead body or something. Once Dad had told them about a tired deer they had picked up on the river. To keep it out of trouble, they had put it in one of the crew member's quarters. When they opened the door a little later, the deer was lying on the bed, his legs sticking out to one side.

It wasn't a dead body this time, though, or even a deer. It was a dog story.

"Got past Lockport, just this side of Romeoville, when Curly—he's on watch—catches this dog in the beam of his searchlight. Half drowned, it was, paddling like it's hardly got the strength to whine. Curly hauls it out with a net, we rub it down with a towel, and a sorrier excuse for a dog you never saw. Had on a collar that said 'Jeepers,' so we called the county police, told them we had this dog, and that we'd be tied up at Lemont for a couple of days."

"What happened?" Jimmy said.

"Well, first off we gave the dog a little soup, see if he could hold it down. After a couple hours, when he seemed to frisk up a bit, we set a plate on the floor—beef with gravy, baked beans, corn, biscuits—same as the rest of us were having, and you should have seen that dog eat! Took his plate away from him once so he could catch his breath, and when we give it back, he lapped the whole thing up. Didn't hear anything from the police, and figured, well now, what are we going to do with this dog? But the day before we pulled out, here come this little girl and her dad in a pickup, all the way from Cicero. Said they'd been going across a bridge one night and something scared the dog. He jumped out the back of the pickup and right into the water. They thought for sure it was the last they'd seen of Jeepers. Well, the current carried him downstream a-ways, but that dog just figured it wasn't his time to go, I guess."

"I liked that story," David said when it was over. "I like happy endings."

Jimmy saw his mother and dad exchange glances.

"Those are the best kind," said Dad. He went over to the candy machine by the lock house and bought a Clark bar each for David and Jimmy.

"That water's high enough, so I've got to get back on," he said. "Those new deckhands don't tie us off right, we'll be halfway to Cairo before the *Herman C.* catches up to us. Seems like every time I get me a new man, I got to work twice as hard." He handed Benjamin back to Mother.

"I've been hearing reports on the radio about how high the Mississippi is," Mother said, worry in her voice.

"Been high every spring for the seven years I've been working on the *Herman C.,*" Dad said, squeezing her arm. "You haven't lost me yet. You give Lois my best wishes now, when she's better. And you take care, David. Bet you won't even be here when I get back from New Orleans. You'll be back in Cincinnati with your ma pitching horseshoes or something."

David gave a little smile, but it didn't seem to stretch very far on his face.

Father bent down even lower, until his eyes were even with David's. "And if you *are* here when I get back, I'm going to take you fishing on the Kankakee River. Okay?"

Jimmy couldn't believe his father had said that. Fishing on the Kankakee had always been their own special time together, his and Dad's. It seemed as though everyone was inviting David right into the family—just begging him to stay as long as he liked.

"'Course, we'd take Jimmy, too," Dad grinned, playfully shaking Jimmy's shoulder. Jimmy didn't say a word. Didn't even smile. He watched while his dad went back through the visitor's gate and on down the canal to where the *Herman C.* waited. Bart Novak hopped up on the lock wall and jumped over onto the lead barge.

After the water gates swung open, Jimmy's dad, using his walkie-talkie, spoke to the pilot back on the towboat. "You're a hundred and fifty feet," he said, watching the numbers that were painted on the wall of the channel as the barge moved through and the front of it reached the markers. "You're three feet off the right wall." The walkie-talkie squealed back at him as Smitty, the pilot, answered.

Jimmy and his mother and David and Benjamin stayed long enough to watch Dad teaching the new deckhand to unhook one barge from another. After the first four barges were in the lock, they were unhooked from the others so that the *Herman C.* could back up, pulling half its load with it. Then the gates of the lock closed, and the water began to drop. It would be about two hours by the time the lock emptied, then filled up again for the last of the tow—two and a half hours, maybe, before the *Herman C.* was finally on its way to the Mississippi.

Mother waved at Dad, then they all went back down to the parking lot.

There wasn't a thing his father couldn't do on a towboat, Jimmy was thinking—even steer it himself, should anything happen to the captain or pilot, steer those barges right through the locks as smooth as anything, he bet. Probably wasn't a thing his father hadn't tried.

He wondered if his dad, when he was younger, had ever gone out at night to ride the railroad bridge without his family knowing. Maybe. He wondered, too, if his dad had ever swum in the limestone quarries around Joliet. Probably not. That was about the most dangerous thing you could do. Just last year a boy had drowned, and Bart Novak had said then that if he ever caught Jimmy near a quarry, he'd tan the seat of his pants.

Jimmy had no plans to swim in a quarry. But Dad hadn't said one word about not riding the railroad bridge. Not one word at all.

8

DAVID'S DREAM

Mother and Aunt Lois's brother, Uncle Sheldon, had flown from Montana to Cincinnati to see how Aunt Lois was doing after her operation. He said he would call Mother twice a day and would stay in Cincinnati until Aunt Lois was "out of the woods," which made Mother feel much better about not being in Cincinnati herself. "Out of the woods," Jimmy knew, meant "out of danger."

When Uncle Sheldon called Wednesday night just before the boys went to bed, he said that Aunt Lois was awake, but she "wasn't out of the woods yet." Thursday morning, when he called, he said she was about the same, but still had a way to go before she was "out of the woods."

"I thought she was in a hospital," David said, trying to figure it out.

"What your Uncle Sheldon means is that there's still a long way to go before she's well again, but every day she'll be a little bit better than the day before," Mother said.

Jimmy wondered if that was really true. Sometimes people said what they knew was true and sometimes they said what they only *hoped* was true.

On the last day of school before spring vacation, the three Thonkers decided to do something that would show just how rough, tough, and terrible the Thonkers could really be.

First they wore their black Thonker T-shirts to class. Next they took a package of straight pins and carefully stitched them into the thick skin on the palms of their left hands. A staple in the thumb wasn't anything compared to a whole row of pins on the palm.

"I guess you boys are practicing to be surgeons?" the teacher said when she saw them. "Take them out."

At recess, though, each boy ate a bug. A live bug. Sam ate an ant, Peter ate a fly, and Jimmy found a brown beetle under a rock in the corner of the playground and bit it in half. He was sure that the legs were still moving when he swallowed it down.

"Oh, gross!" some of the girls screamed.

"Neat!" said one of the boys.

David just sat with his hands over his mouth, not saying a word.

When school was out, some of the third grade boys followed along behind the Thonkers, wanting to know if they could join the club.

Jimmy said they weren't taking any new members

49

right now, and he hinted that there was something else the Thonkers were going to do that was so rough, tough, and terrible they couldn't even talk about it until it was over.

"Wow!" said one of the boys.

It was a great way to start spring vacation.

The only problem with having meetings in the Novaks' garage after school was that Peter took music lessons on Tuesdays and Sam took lessons on Fridays. Joliet was proud of its school bands. Peter played the French horn and Sam played the trombone, and both of them had older brothers who played in Joliet high school bands as well.

Jimmy's family wasn't very musical, however. Mother could sing a little, but Jimmy and his dad sounded awful. So while Sam went off for his Friday lesson and Peter was home practicing, Jimmy spent the time in the garage, getting it ready for a whole week of spring vacation.

He had just pushed an old mattress over a little further to make room for the folding chairs Peter had brought when there was a knock at the door.

"Who is it?" Jimmy called.

"Me," answered David.

"Private club," said Jimmy. "Sorry."

"Well, your mom said for me to give you this."

Jimmy got up on a chair and looked out the garage door window. David was standing there holding a sack of plastic cups and plates and a couple of boxes of crackers.

Jimmy hopped down and opened the door, and David simply walked inside and set the things on the table. What the heck, Jimmy thought, Sam and Peter weren't there anyway; it wouldn't hurt to let David look around.

"Wow!" David said. He was staring at the "Rough, Tough, and Terrible" sign on the wall. "This is really nice."

"Nice" wasn't exactly the word Jimmy would have used to describe their clubhouse, but it was okay.

"Everybody heard how you put pins in your hands," David said. "Would I have to do that to be a Thonker?"

Jimmy almost laughed out loud. David couldn't be tough if his life depended on it. "Don't worry about it," he said. "We aren't taking any new members."

"Could I just sit here and watch for a while?" David wanted to know. "I won't touch anything."

"I guess," Jimmy told him.

David sat down in one of the folding chairs, swinging his legs back and forth.

"You know what some kids called me today at school?" he said finally.

Jimmy took the plastic cups and set them on a shelf. Then the spoons and plates. "What?" he asked.

David stared down at his feet. "Sissy Pants. They thought I'd cry and I almost did, but I didn't."

"Why'd they call you that?"

"We were playing Red Rover at recess, and I was the last one to be chosen and one of the boys said, 'Looks like I have to take old Sissy Pants.'"

Jimmy wasn't too sure how to answer. If *he* was playing Red Rover, he sure wouldn't want David on his team.

"Oh, they were just teasing," he said at last. "It wouldn't hurt to toughen yourself up a little, though. Don't whine so much. Stuff like that." And then, changing the subject, he asked, "How's your mom doing? Any news?"

"She's about the same," David said. He continued swinging his feet, studying the "Rough, Tough, and Terrible" sign some more. "Do you ever have scary dreams?" he asked suddenly.

"Sometimes," said Jimmy.

"I had a bad dream last night," David told him. "I dreamed I was in the woods and couldn't find my way out."

"That's scary?" Jimmy said, and actually laughed. "That isn't *half* scary! Not unless there were bears in there with you."

"There weren't any bears," said David, "but in my dream, my mom was lost in the woods, too, and *she* couldn't find her way out, either."

Jimmy didn't answer then. Somehow, looking at David, the dream did seem a little scary after all.

9

THE LIFE

Over the weekend, March became April, and Jimmy and his friends moved into their clubhouse.

Marsha Evans came over to give Jimmy's mother a permanent and brought an old blanket for the boys to use. Whenever George Evans and Jimmy's father were working on the towboat together, Marsha and Mother got together to sew or bake or to do their weekly shopping. Jimmy ran back and forth between the house and the garage, carrying down comic books and clothes and games.

"That clubhouse is going to have everything!" Marsha laughed as she put another roller in Mother's hair and wound it up tight. "Listen, Carol, maybe *we* should go live in the garage for a week and let the boys take care of the house."

"And let them take care of the babies, too!" Mother joked. Marsha's baby, Kevin, was in the playpen with Benjamin, and they were hitting each other with the Easter bunnies they had been given already.

"Where's David?" Mother asked, without moving her head, when Jimmy returned to the house one last time. Half of her hair was already rolled up in curlers.

"Watching TV," Jimmy said, and went back outside before she could say any more.

The Thonkers put the old blanket on the mattress and some pillows on top of that. Then they stacked their comic books, put the games on a shelf, and sat down in Peter's folding chairs to eat the sausage sandwiches that Mrs. Angelino had sent over for their lunch.

A whole week of spring vacation stretched out before them and seemed to make them silly. They shook their cans of pop up and down and sprayed each other when they opened the tabs.

"Man, this is the life!" said Jimmy at last, sprawling out on the mattress. "I wish I could just live out here till David goes back to Cincinnati."

"If I had a cousin like him, I don't know what I'd do," said Sam.

"I don't see how you stand it," Peter added. "David's a real nerd."

"Yeah," Jimmy agreed. "You wouldn't *believe* the things that kid has to do before he goes to bed at night."

"Like what?" asked Peter.

Jimmy sat up on one elbow and grinned. "Well, first he takes a bath with his PT boat. . . ."

Peter started to giggle.

"Then he brushes his teeth with his Big Bird tooth-brush. . . ."

Sam joined in the laughter.

"Then he puts on his Bambi pajamas and walks in the bedroom like this. . . ." Jimmy got up from the mattress and showed them the way David walked bare-foot down the hall, carefully picking up each foot and setting it down as though any moment he might see a bug.

"And then," Jimmy added, as the boys' laughter became howls, "then he lays out all his clothes like this . . . his shoes here, socks here, shirt here. . . . I asked him once what would happen if he didn't lay out everything the night before, and he said"—now Jimmy himself was laughing—"he said that he might forget to put something on, and that once he went to school without his underpants."

Sam and Peter yelped with laughter, and it was half a minute before they could talk again.

"Just keep him away from here," said Sam. "We ought to put a sign on the door: 'No Nerds Allowed.' "

"Yeah," said Peter. " 'No Nosy Nerds Allowed.' "

" 'No Nosy Nerds in Bambi Pajamas,' " Sam went on, and somehow Jimmy wished that he hadn't said anything about the pajamas and the Big Bird tooth-brush. He was glad that he hadn't said anything about the teddy bear.

There were all sorts of places to hide in the alley that night when the boys went out to play kick the can. They stayed outside until Sam fell over a box of trash and it was simply too dark to see any longer. Then they went back inside their clubhouse and turned on the light.

The only problem with living in the garage was that their food didn't stay very cold. Their cans of pop tasted like warm tea, so Jimmy went up to the house to get the ice chest that he and his dad took with them on camping trips.

Mother was sitting on the couch giving Benjamin a bottle and reading a story to David. She looked very different because her hair was all curly, like Marsha's.

"How are things going down there in the club-house?" she asked, as Jimmy rummaged about in the closet. "You won't be afraid out there all night, will you?"

"Heck no!" Jimmy answered.

"Well, remember that tomorrow's Easter. We'll be going to Mass."

"Yeah," Jimmy said. "But I'm going back out in the garage as soon as we get home from church. We just might decide to sleep out there all summer, the three of us."

"What about rats?" asked David.

Jimmy pulled his head out of the closet and slowly turned around. "Rats? We don't have any rats, do we, Mom?"

"Not that I know of," his mother said. "We've had plenty of mice out there, though."

"Rats live near rivers," David said.

Jimmy thrust his head back in the closet again and finally found the ice chest. "Well, if there were going to be rats, we'd have seen them by now," he told his cousin. "Besides, there's no way for them to get in."

"Rats can chew through anything," David went on. "There was a man who lived on the seventeenth floor of an apartment building and some rats came in the basement and chewed through the wall and climbed up the wires and came out through his medicine cabinet and ate his cat."

"Baloney!" said Jimmy, bolting straight up. "That's a bunch of baloney, David."

David just shook his head. "I saw it on television," he said.

Jimmy went back in his bedroom to get his flashlight, and while he was there he looked up "rat" in the children's encyclopedia that his grandfather had given him at Christmas.

"Rats," said the encyclopedia, "are terrible pests. They carry disease and their sharp teeth can gnaw through wood, plaster, wire, glass, and even soft metal such as lead. . . ."

Jimmy swallowed. Then he picked up the ice chest and flashlight, stopped in the kitchen for a tray of ice cubes, and went on outside. He held the flashlight so he could see where he stepped. Once he was sure he saw a blade of grass move, and he stopped. There was nothing there, however, so he climbed over the fence and dropped to the alley below.

The boys lay on the mattress, reading comic books and eating cheese crackers. They had already polished off the supper Jimmy's mother made for them and finally decided to tell ghost stories. They latched the door from the inside, turned out the light, and crawled under the blanket.

Sam told the story of "The Golden Arm," which Jimmy had already heard, and then Peter told the one about the butcher who was out of liver, so he went to the graveyard and cut out the liver of a dead man. Jimmy had heard that one too. "I want my liver! I want my liver," the dead man kept saying as he came up the stairs to kill the butcher. It wasn't very scary, though, after you'd heard it a zillion times.

So when it was his turn to tell a story, Jimmy told about this man who was allergic to mice and rats, so he bought himself this big cat and moved to the very top floor of a high-rise apartment building. And then one night this giant rat with teeth like a power saw climbed up out of the river, all dripping with slime, and came down the alley, *pit, pat, pit, pat,* and squeezed through a window in the basement of the high rise, *squish, squash, squish, squash,* and ate a hole in the wall, *crack, crunch, crack, crunch,* and climbed up the electric wires, *scritch, scratch, scritch, scratch,* and gnawed through the back of the medicine cabinet on the very top floor and came out in the bathroom and ate the man's cat (here Jimmy gave a horrible yeowl like a cat being devoured) and then, the huge, horrible, slimy rat with teeth like a power saw crept into the bedroom where the man was sleeping. . . .

By the time Jimmy had finished the story, Sam had moved six inches closer on one side of him and Peter had moved six inches closer on the other.

"That was a *good* story, Jimmy!" Sam said. "That was better than 'The Golden Arm.'"

It was some time before anyone went to sleep. At last, however, Jimmy heard the steady sounds of Peter's breathing, and finally Sam drifted off, too. But Jimmy didn't feel very tired. His dad might be in bed already, though, he was thinking. When Dad worked on the towboat, he had six hours on duty, then six hours off, day after day. You kept strange hours and ate your meals at odd times on a towboat.

Sometimes, when Jimmy woke up in the middle of the night, he liked to think that right that very minute his dad might be awake—be on duty as night watch out there on the river, looking after things, making sure the boat was okay.

His dad always said that his favorite place of all to work was on the very first barge in the tow, the lead barge. "Riding the head," he called it. Way up there, he always said, a long way from the boat and its engine, the river was quiet. The barge moved through the water without any sound at all, and the landscape rolled by on either side like a picture show.

If Dad were on watch tonight, he'd be working by flashlight. You always had to be careful when you worked on a barge in the dark, Dad had told Jimmy. The first rule they always taught a new deckhand was

"Never step in a shadow," and Jimmy knew why: because the shadow might be the space between two barges or maybe an open hatch, not a shadow at all. It might be a step right off into the water.

There was a soft, scraping kind of noise from somewhere in the garage. Jimmy bolted up on one elbow and listened.

"Peter!" he said, nudging his friend. "I think we've got rats."

"That's not rats," Peter murmured sleepily.

"Listen!" Jimmy said, and waited. The noise came again. It sounded like a rat with sharp teeth gnawing through the wall of the garage, crunching and biting and nibbling and gnawing, making its way closer and closer to where the boys lay on the mattress. Or maybe it was an escaped convict looking for a hideout—slowly picking at the latch through the crack in the door with a switchblade.

"That's not rats," Peter said again. "That's the door shifting back and forth on its hinges. Every time the wind blows, you hear it."

Jimmy listened again. For a few minutes all was still. Then he heard the wind stirring and the sound came again, just like Peter said. It was only the soft scraping of the door.

"You're right," Jimmy said, and lay back down. But it was a long time before he was asleep.

10

SCOUTING THE BRIDGE

On Monday, after playing darts on the wall of the garage, hiding each other's sneakers, and holding a contest to see who could belch the loudest, the boys made plans for riding the railroad bridge.

"Okay," said Jimmy. "Here's what we'll do. Saturday right after dinner, I'll ask Mom if we can use the Monopoly set. It takes hours to play a whole game, and she'll figure we're out here all the while."

Sam and Peter nodded.

"What we've got to do between now and then," Jimmy went on, "is figure out the shortest way to get to the railroad bridge so we won't be gone any longer than we have to. We've got to ride over there and scout it out."

"*Now?*" Sam asked.

61

Jimmy nodded. "Now."

"My bike has a flat tire," said Sam.

"Mine has a broken chain," said Peter.

Jimmy looked at the other boys disgustedly. "I thought you guys were supposed to be ready for anything! I thought you guys were *Thonkers!*"

Both Sam and Peter reddened.

"I'll fix mine tomorrow," Sam said.

"Well, we're going anyway," Jimmy told them. "We'll walk."

"All the way down to the railroad bridge?" Peter gasped.

"All the way," said Jimmy. "Let's move."

They got up, turned off Sam's transistor radio, opened the door, and walked right smack into David.

"You've been spying on us!" Jimmy said angrily.

"No, I haven't! I was just waiting for you to come out," said David. He was wearing a pair of plaid trousers that his mother must have chosen for him and an orange sweatshirt with the picture of a panda on the front.

"I'll bet you heard everything we said," Sam told him.

"All I heard was the radio," said David.

"So what do you want?" Jimmy asked.

David shrugged and stuck his hands in his pockets. "I just wanted to see what you guys were doing. Benjamin threw up on the rug and I can't stand looking at throw-up. Aunt Carol sent me out here."

"Well, you can't come with us," Peter told him. "We've got things to do."

"Can I help?" David asked.

"No way," said Sam.

Jimmy was a little worried about leaving David there by himself, however. David might go in the garage and mess everything up, just because they wouldn't take him with them.

"Listen, David, you want some m&m's?" Jimmy asked. He took a little sack from his pocket and gave it to David.

"Thanks," David said.

"You can play with my Matchbox cars if you want," Jimmy added. "They're in a box under my bed."

"Okay," said David, and ate an m&m.

"Nerd City," said Sam as soon as they had turned the corner and David was out of sight. "People who buy kids clothes like that ought to go to jail."

"Yeah, it's probably his mother's fault," Peter agreed. "And did you see his *sneakers*? With green laces?"

"Oh, he's not so bad, really," Jimmy said, uncomfortable at the way his friends were talking about David, even though he had said worse things himself.

By the time the boys had gone another block, they'd forgotten Jimmy's cousin. The names of the streets in this part of Joliet seemed to describe the city itself— Granite Street, Marble Street, Lime, Stone, and Bridge streets. As soon as they reached Marble, they made the turn, crossed Broadway, and went down to Bluff Street, where they followed it along the canal.

It was still some distance to the bridge, however—farther than they had realized. Where they could, they walked beside the concrete wall of the canal. Sometimes they had to cut back to the road again to go around a building, but finally, there it stood, the railroad bridge, straight ahead—the two heavy black shafts at either end, holding the roadbed high between them.

"Fifty minutes," Peter said, checking his watch. "We'll make a lot better time on our bikes."

"Yeah," Sam agreed. "Let's say fifteen minutes to get here and fifteen to get back. And then however long it takes to wait for a train to come along."

As the boys walked through the weeds, the bridge seemed far larger than Jimmy had imagined. He had actually never been this close to it before, though he had seen it often when his parents drove by on Railroad Street on this side of the river, or Water Street on the other.

The first thing you noticed about the bridges in Joliet were the black and white stripes of the huge counterweights. On the drawbridges, the counterweights were up, keeping the roadbed down until a boat came by. But on the railroad bridge, they were down, holding the span of track in the air so that boats could go by underneath. When a train was coming, the counterweights moved up and the roadbed, with the railroad tracks on it, came down, lining up perfectly with the tracks on either side.

It wasn't the counterweights that Jimmy was studying now, however, but the edge of the platform high overhead where he would be standing on Saturday night—he and Sam and Peter together. Not that high up, of course.

"How long do you suppose the bridge stays down after a train goes by?" Sam asked finally.

Jimmy didn't really know. "Not very long," he said. "A few seconds, maybe. We've got to get on the moment the train passes."

"What if we get on but don't jump off and the bridge goes all the way back up?" Peter wondered. "Would we be stuck up there forever?"

"We'd just better not let that happen," Jimmy said. "We'd have to climb down somehow, and the bridge tender would see us, and boy, would we catch it when we got home!"

They moved up onto the wooden walkway that ran along one side of the bridge supports. In the little yellow house on the other side of the canal, they could see the bridge tender looking over at them. He rested his arms on the window ledge, watched them a while, then spit into the water.

"We'd better quit staring at the bridge," Jimmy whispered. "He'll know we've got ideas." He went out a little farther on the walkway and threw a stone into the water. Then Sam and Peter did it, too—just three boys out on a fine spring day throwing rocks into the canal. First they tried to see who could throw the farthest. Jimmy picked up a flat stone and tried to make it skip the surface the way Dad had taught him to do last year on the Kankakee, but he was up too high. The bridge tender finally pulled his head back inside his window and picked up a newspaper.

"Whew!" said Jimmy.

They stood looking down the canal, hoping for the sight of a boat, but nothing was moving at all.

Plunk. Something landed in the water behind them. Jimmy turned around.

There stood David down on the bank, a fistful of stones in his hand, throwing them one at a time into the canal.

11

DRESSING DAVID

David!" yelled Jimmy.

"You followed us!" Sam said.

"I'm not hurting anything," David told them.

Jimmy, Sam, and Peter looked at each other. If their mothers knew that they were there at the canal, the boys would be grounded for the rest of the week.

"Does Mom know where you went?" Jimmy asked.

David shook his head and threw another stone. Then he moved over and peered cautiously into the water.

"Let's go home," said Jimmy disgustedly. Nobody said much till they reached the Novaks' yard, then Jimmy walked halfway up to the house with David.

"Now listen," he said, "you'd better not say a word to Mom about us being down by the canal."

"What's so secret?" David asked.

"Just don't tell," Jimmy repeated.

"Can I be a Thonker if I don't?"

"Don't tell!" Jimmy warned.

"David?" called Mother from inside. "I've been *wondering* where you were."

"He was with us, Mom," Jimmy said quickly.

"Well, you tell me when you're taking David somewhere for very long, Jimmy. I want to know."

"Okay," said Jimmy, and went back down to the garage.

"You think he'll tell?" Sam asked.

"He'd better not!" Jimmy said.

For the rest of the afternoon, he expected that any moment his mother would call him up to the house. Somehow she would question David about where he had been, and somehow David would give it away. Two o'clock became three, however, and three became four. When Jimmy went up at last to get some supper for the others, Mother cheerfully dished up three bowls of chili and put them on a tray.

"You guys finding things to do out there?" she asked.

David glanced up at Jimmy, grinned, and went on eating.

"Sure," said Jimmy. "Lots." *How about that!* he was thinking. The kid *could* keep a secret!

On Tuesday, both Sam and Peter went home to practice their music lessons, so Jimmy went up to the house. Marsha Evans had come over again with her baby, and she and Mother were making a big stuffed clown for Kevin's first birthday.

"How you doing, Jimmy?" Marsha said as she cut out the clown pattern on the dining room table. "How many birthdays has *your* dad missed, anyway? I'm just curious."

Jimmy shrugged. "I think he was here for my sixth."

"Your first, your fourth, and your sixth," said Mother, weaving her needle in and out. "He missed all the others."

"That's just what I'm beginning to find out," Marsha sighed. "George missed being with us at Easter, he's going to miss Kevin's birthday. . . . He's only been working on that towboat for a few months, Carol, and he's already missed two special days!"

Mother gave her a little smile. "You know what you do, Marsha? You celebrate twice, that's all. Once on the day itself, and again when George gets home."

"Really?" Marsha picked up the scissors again. "Well, I guess that's not too bad, huh, Jimmy? If your dad's a boatman, you get twice as many birthdays."

Jimmy just laughed and went on down the hall.

David was in Jimmy's room, making a get-well card for his mother. He was sitting on the trundle bed, using Jimmy's bed as a desk, and there were scraps of paper and little dried-up bits of paste all over the bedspread.

"Guess what?" he said. "Mom's out of intensive care!"

"That's great!" Jimmy said. He wondered if he

should thank David for not saying anything to Mom about going to the canal. Then he decided perhaps he shouldn't bring it up again, and maybe David would forget about it altogether.

He sat down on the radiator and looked at his cousin. This time David was wearing red-and-yellow-checked pants and a red polo shirt with a yellow stripe down each sleeve. They matched! David looked like one of those boys in the Sears catalog with matching clothes, the kind of boys who wore sweaters around their shoulders with the sleeves tied in front. Jimmy had never in his life seen a real boy with a sweater tied around his shoulders except in catalogs.

"David," Jimmy said at last, "who chooses your clothes?"

"Mom," David said, without even looking up.

"She ever ask you what the other guys wear?"

"Huh-uh," David said, pressing down hard with the purple crayon. "I just wear whatever she gets."

"What would you *like* to wear?" asked Jimmy.

David shrugged. "I don't know."

David looked awfully small somehow, Jimmy thought, sitting there on the trundle bed, feet tucked under him, one of his green shoelaces dangling. He thought of how the other children must have teased David when he walked into that second grade classroom for the first time in his reindeer sweater.

Jimmy opened his closet door. On a hook near the back was a pair of jeans he had outgrown the summer before. He took them out and put them on the bed. Then he opened the bottom drawer of his dresser, where he kept his very favorite T-shirt with a picture of King Kong on it. Mother had put it in the dryer by mistake and it had shrunk. He put that on the bed beside the jeans.

"David," he said, "how would you like some new clothes?"

David turned around and Jimmy held up the shirt.

"What's that gorilla doing?" David asked, staring at the picture.

"Destroying New York City," said Jimmy. "Haven't you ever heard of King Kong?"

David began to grin. "Neat!" he said.

"Well, you can have it. The jeans, too."

"Thanks!" David got up and unbuckled his belt. His pants slid down to his ankles, and he took them off. He pulled Jimmy's jeans up his skinny legs, then put on the shirt. The jeans were a little big, but a belt would hold them up.

"Wow!" he said as he stood in front of the mirror.

"One more thing," said Jimmy. "You've got to get rid of those green shoelaces."

Dutifully, David pulled the laces out of his sneakers, and Jimmy gave him a new pair from his drawer.

"Mom," Jimmy said that night when David was in the bathtub, "how come David turned out like he is?"

Mother was sitting at the kitchen table writing a letter to Dad. "What do you mean?" she asked.

"A weirdo," said Jimmy.

"Please don't use that word, Jimmy."

"A baby, then. He wears weird clothes, he doesn't

eat half the stuff you put in his lunch, he whimpers when he gets hit in kickball. . . ."

Mother put down her pen. "I guess that's Lois's fault, but it's not as though she *meant* to make him different."

"Well, she did a pretty good job of it by accident then," Jimmy said. "The kids in his class call him Sissy Pants—the way he dresses, the way he complains."

Mother was really listening now. "I suppose," she said finally, "that when Lois's husband died, she babied David because he's all the family she's got there in Cincinnati."

"He's not *normal*, Mom! *Nobody* wears plaid pants to school! Plaid pants and panda shirts and green shoe-laces!"

"That's what Lois sent with him."

"Well, he's wearing some clothes of mine now. At least let him wear my stuff to school. Okay?"

Mother began to smile. "You're the boss," she said.

It was what Mom often said when Dad was away on the boat—as though Jimmy was now man of the house. It made him feel a little scared and a little special, both at the same time. He wondered if David ever felt that way.

"Here," Mother said, handing him a piece of paper, folded over twice. "You got a letter today from your dad. He tucked it inside a letter to me."

Jimmy smiled. He always liked it when Dad wrote to him. He filled a saucer with chocolate grahams and took them into the living room to read the letter.

12

A LETTER FROM DAD

Jimmy laughed out loud when he unfolded the piece
of paper, because Bart Novak always drew a little cartoon at the top of his letters to Jimmy. He had been
in the navy once and had a tatoo on the back of his
hand. The cartoons were always about a man in an
old cap with a tatoo on the back of his hand. The man
was supposed to be Dad, but he always looked a little
like Popeye.

This time the man was standing with one foot
on the end of one barge and one foot on the end of
another, and there were ripples in the water to show
that the barges were moving away from each other.
Dad had drawn little squiggles beside the man's knees
to show that his legs were shaking. There were drops
of sweat flying out from the man's face, and he was
saying, "Help!!!" Jimmy giggled some more.

Dear Jimmy,

How's my buddy? How are you guys liking your camp-out there in the garage? Thought of you yesterday when we went through Ottawa.

Folks in Ottawa know when Smitty's piloting a boat, because he always grabs the whistle cord and sends out a couple blasts as we pass the junior high. Teachers let Smitty's kids come to the window and wave at their old man. Makes me wish we passed by your school on our way through Joliet. I'd run up to the pilothouse and make that whistle cord dance, let me tell you.

It sure does feel good to hit this bunk. We had to stop three times because of fog last night. Cold as a witch's toenail out here on the river, and we had to pick up another barge. A grain barge, this time. Now we've got nine barges in tow, and getting them through those bridges was one heck of a job.

First one was easy. You get a straight-in shot and lots of room between piers. You could do it yourself, Jimmy, clean as a whistle, I'll bet. But that Franklin Street span is only 121 feet wide, and the third's out there on the river the craziest angle you ever saw. You almost got to jackknife to shoehorn your way through, but Smitty did it.

Got a new cook this trip—man from Arkansas. Makes the best biscuits you ever want to taste. Big supper last night, which is what we needed

*with all that work ahead of us. Baked chicken
and dressing, sweet potatoes, kernel corn, cauli-
flower, biscuits, cole slaw, green beans, about a
dozen other vegetables I can't remember, and chocolate pie. A cake, too. And lemonade, along with
the coffee. Be fat as a walrus if I didn't work so
hard. Too bad I can't save some of this chow for
David—stout him up a little.*

*Can't hardly keep my eyes open another min-
ute, so I'm going to give this letter to George and
he'll hand it to the man on the supply boat when
they bring out our groceries tomorrow. Hope you
and David are hitting it off okay.*

Big, big bear hug,
Dad

Jimmy imagined himself in the pilothouse, steering a boat like the *Herman C.* If he were ever on board
and all the men suddenly got sick or something—too
sick to even get up out of their bunks—could he do
it? For a few miles, maybe.

He knew that when you are going down a river,
you have to keep the black channel markers on your
right and the red markers on your left so you don't
run into a sandbar, and that when you go *up* a river,
it's just the opposite. And he knew that you put the
engine in reverse to help swing the barges around a
sharp curve, but he wouldn't know how to do it, not

even if he had to. Dad could, though, he bet.

Jimmy tried to figure out just when his father would reach New Orleans. Saturday, probably. It took about ten days to go from Joliet to New Orleans, if everything went all right. "Ten days at twelve miles an hour," his dad used to say. "That's the life!"

Jimmy was feeling a little bad about the way he hadn't said good-bye to his father there at the Brandon Road lock because he was jealous of Dad talking about taking David fishing on the Kankakee.

He got up from the sofa, tore a page out of his school tablet, and went out in the kitchen.

"Are you writing to Dad, too?" Mother said, as he sat down at the table across from her.

He nodded. *If I mail it tomorrow,* he thought, *it should be waiting for Dad when he gets to New Orleans.*

13

STORM

On Tuesday night, things began to get a little wild out in the clubhouse. Soon after Jimmy fell asleep, he was awakened by a faraway thumping sound overhead. He opened his eyes. This was no door shifting in the wind; this was footsteps on the earth over the garage. He poked Sam. Sam had heard them, too. Both boys lay without moving. Someone was definitely up there. An escaped convict, maybe, looking for a place to hide.

"Wake Peter," Sam breathed.

Jimmy reached over to nudge Peter. Peter was gone. Then they knew. Jimmy and Sam crept out of the garage, turned the water hose on Peter, who was horsing around overhead, and Peter—yelping and braying—leaped down on Sam there in the alley. Lights came on in several houses and one neighbor called Jimmy's mother to complain.

On Wednesday night after the others fell asleep, it was Sam who crept outside, stood on a box below the garage door window, and, holding a flashlight just under his chin, tapped on the pane and made the most terrible face. Peter and Jimmy woke to see what looked like a floating head leering at them. This time a gravel battle followed in the alley, with trash can lids for shields, and Mother said if the boys didn't quiet down, they'd have to sleep in the house. The Thonkers quieted down.

On Thursday morning, when Jimmy went up to the house to get cereal for the other Thonkers, Uncle Sheldon called to say that Aunt Lois was feeling a whole lot better, and that David could talk to her on the phone.

Jimmy had never seen his cousin look as happy as he did then—more like a kid and less like a little old man with worry lines on his face. David was grinning so widely it looked as though even his ears were stretching. Jimmy hadn't realized before just how much David had been worrying. It was only when he saw him smile that he knew it for sure.

He took Benjamin out of the kitchen so that David could talk to Aunt Lois on the phone, and while he bounced Benjy around on the couch, he could hear David's excited voice, asking his mother if she got his card and telling her about the things he'd been doing in Joliet.

"Jimmy, would you like to say a few words to Aunt Lois before I talk with her?" Mother called. Jimmy put Benjamin in his playpen and went to the phone in the kitchen.

"Hi," he said. "We're glad you're better, Aunt Lois."

Her voice sounded weak and far away, but she said, "It's such a nice feeling to know that you and your mother are taking good care of David for me. He's always liked you so much, Jimmy. I really appreciate it."

"I'm glad to do it," Jimmy said. He wondered why people lied on the telephone. Well, maybe it wasn't a *complete* lie. He didn't *hate* David, after all. He was glad he could give him some decent clothes to wear, but he didn't want David hanging around forever.

As the Thonkers ate their Wheat Chex in the garage later, Sam said, "What's David eating? Cocoa Puffsies?"

Peter whooped. "Fruitie Loopies," he laughed.

"Hey, give him a break," Jimmy said.

Sam stopped chewing. "Don't tell me you're going soft on David?"

"Who's soft?" said Jimmy. *"You* eat Fruit Loops, too, Sam. I saw some in your cupboard."

Sam reddened. "They were my sister's," he said.

"Yeah, sure!" said Peter, and they all laughed.

It was not very pleasant in the garage that morning. There were dark swirling clouds in the sky, and the air had a heavy, damp feel to it. Even the mattress and blanket had smelled musty when the boys got up that morning. Some sort of fungus appeared on one of the inside walls of the garage.

"I feel like a mushroom," Peter said at last.

"The TV said there were going to be thunderstorms," Sam told him.

"As long as it doesn't rain Saturday night," said Jimmy. "If it rains then, that bridge is going to be slippery. Dad always talks about how slippery metal is when it's wet." He pulled the collar of his jacket up and thrust his hands in his pockets. It really *was* chilly in the garage. "You want some hot chocolate?" he said finally. "I'll go up to the house and make some."

The kitchen felt warm and dry when Jimmy walked in. David was sitting at the table finishing a plate of scrambled eggs, and Mother was feeding Benjy his oatmeal.

"We've got tickets for the magic show on Saturday, Jimmy," she reminded him. "Don't forget."

Jimmy slowly put down the cocoa box in his hand. *Saturday?* "What time Saturday?" he asked.

"The afternoon matinee," said his mother. "Marsha's coming over to watch Benjamin while we're gone, then we're all going to celebrate little Kevin's birthday."

Whew, Jimmy said under his breath. There would still be plenty of time to go to the railroad bridge.

It was too wet out that night to play in the alley, so after Sam told a ghost story and then Peter, Jimmy told the scariest story they had ever heard. In fact, it was the scariest story that *Jimmy* had ever heard. It was about this mad killer who escaped from Stateville and he was hitchhiking along the road and this man picked him up and the convict shot him and cut his body up in pieces and put each part in a different box and mailed them all over the country. People would get a box in the mail and open it up and there would be a bloody foot or a finger. Policemen everywhere were looking for him.

"What happened?" Peter asked. "Don't stop there, Jimmy! What happened? Did they catch him!"

"Nope," said Jimmy.

"He just went on shooting people and cutting them up and mailing them all around?" Sam squeaked.

Jimmy thought for a minute. Outside the rain was streaming down the windows of the garage. "This convict was really smart, and whenever the police thought they had him trapped, he escaped. He had all this money from the people he had killed and robbed, so he bought this big house with a swimming pool right beside the ocean, and one day there was a hurricane and a shark was washed out of the ocean into the swimming pool and it had babies and one of the baby sharks swam up a water pipe and into the convict's house and into his toilet and the next time the convict went to the bathroom the shark pulled him down into the toilet and through the water pipe and into the pool and all the sharks tore him to pieces and the water turned red."

"Gross!" said Peter.

"That's the most horrible story I ever heard!" said Sam. "I'm going to tell it to the other guys at school."

Jimmy smiled to himself in the dark.

By Friday the rain came down in torrents. It rushed over the grass in the backyard like a water slide, and oozed through the cinder blocks in the back wall of the garage. There was a steady *drip, drip* from a leak overhead, and the graham crackers on the shelf were so damp that when Jimmy picked one up between thumb and finger, it bent like a banana peel.

"I think I'd better get home and practice my trombone lesson," said Sam.

"Yeah," said Peter. "I've got some practicing to do, too."

"Well, why don't we all stay home tonight, then," Jimmy suggested. "We can meet here again tomorrow night at seven-thirty, ready to go."

"Rain or shine?" asked Peter.

"Rain or shine," Jimmy said. "Remember to wear dark clothes—socks, shirts, everything. Anything light will show up."

For a few hours the rain stopped, and then another storm moved in. Jimmy took as hot a shower as he could stand. The smell of the garage seemed to have stuck inside his nostrils. Even under the shower, he thought he could smell the musty blanket, their sneakers, the mold on the walls. Suddenly he heard a noise that sounded like an explosion.

He turned off the water and listened. Through the bathroom window he could see a flash of lightning, and a few seconds later, when thunder crashed and boomed, it sounded as though there was a war going on in the living room. Jimmy dried, pulled on his jeans, and went down the hall.

Mother was sitting in the big chair by the lamp with Benjamin on her lap. David was on the couch holding a saucepan in one hand and a lid in the other. He looked as though he had been crying.

There was another flash of lightning.

"Here it comes, David! Get ready!" Mother said gaily, laughing and hugging Benjy to her.

Ka-BOOM! went the thunder. Both Benjamin and David jumped, and David banged the lid and the saucepan together as hard as he could. Benjamin gave a startled giggle.

"What's going on?" Jimmy asked.

"I'm afraid of storms," David explained.

The TV was going in one corner of the room, but no one was listening. Lightning flashed again, and again the thunder cracked.

Crash! went the saucepan and lid.

This time Benjy laughed out loud. David tried to laugh, but his voice was shaky.

What a baby! Jimmy thought, and went on down the hall.

The rain came steadily, streaking down the window so hard that it was almost impossible to see out, making a pond of the side yard. The television in the living room was still blaring.

"Thunderstorms in the Midwest with some flooding," the announcer was saying. "Possibility of tornadoes in the south and southeast. In the western states, cloudy and cool. . . ."

Gradually the thunder grew fainter and fainter, and by the time Jimmy had read a comic book, it was only a faint rumble in the distance.

David came in and sat down on the trundle bed.

"How come you're scared of a little storm?" Jimmy asked.

"Because they're *scary*," David said.

"It's not as though you were outside," Jimmy told him. "Sometimes you're sort of a baby about things, David."

"You never know about lightning," said David. "There was this boy who was sound asleep under the covers in his own bed and the lightning came down and hit a tree and the tree hit the front porch and lightning came in over the wires and out of the electric socket beside the boy's bed and set his sheets on fire."

"That's crazy, David!"

"It's true! I heard it over the radio!"

"Well, if it ever happened, it's one in a million."

"So am I," David sighed. "That's what Mom always says about me. I'm one in a million."

You can say that again! Jimmy thought. *You're about the biggest weirdo I ever saw in my life!*

But he wasn't really thinking about David. He was thinking about the weather forecast. If it was still raining on Saturday, a railroad bridge was about the most dangerous place you could be.

14

SHOWTIME

When Jimmy woke up to the sound of rain on Saturday, he didn't think he could stand it. There was no thunder, no sudden gusts of wind, just the steady beat of rain on the roof and window—the kind of rain that could go on all day.

They *had* to ride the railroad bridge. Sam, it turned out, had told a few other boys in their class what they were going to do. He hadn't said when, but the whole third grade would be waiting to hear. There were no certain times when freight trains crossed the bridge, but usually you could count on one on Saturday evenings when the commuter trains weren't running. If the boys didn't get to do it this Saturday night, they'd probably have to wait a whole week, and the other guys would tease them about chickening out.

David was already up eating pancakes when Jimmy came glumly into the kitchen. It was ten o'clock and there was another letter from Dad propped against his juice glass.

"Aren't you the lucky boy!" Mother said. "Two letters in one week! David got one, too."

"Mine's from Mom!" David said brightly. "She's going home from the hospital in two weeks, and she says I can come back then."

"That's great," Jimmy said. Any other time, that would have been the happiest news he could think of, but his mind was only on the rain and whether or not it would stop.

He drank his juice, then took Dad's letter back into the bedroom. At the top of the page was the cartoon man sitting out on the deck of the towboat. His right hand was rubbing his stomach in pleasure and his left hand was holding something to eat. The cartoon man was licking his lips and saying, "I'm in luck! Got the very last one of Charlie's buttermilk biscuits!" and there, over his head, was a seagull, all ready to dive and snatch the biscuit away.

St. Louis, Missouri

Hey, Buddy!

We're on the Mississippi now, and you should see this river today—high and churning with current. The Herman C. *doesn't mind it one bit,*

87

though. Last night Smitty had to hold her rock-steady in the boil for two hours while workboats hustled out one barge and tacked on five more. Grain, again.

St. Louis doesn't look like much when you go through here in the daytime, but at night she's all lit up, lights of every color. Looks like Hong Kong.

We're heading for Cairo now, and the river's wide. Looks like two rivers, almost, because up river a-ways, where the Missouri pours in, the water's a sort of chocolate brown color, and it keeps to itself along the Missouri bank. The old Miss, though, battleship gray, flows down along the Illinois side—like the two waters aren't having nothing to do with each other. All that'll change when we get to Cairo where the Ohio River flows in.

The boat rides easy—makes you think there's nothing to it. Like a peaceful old farm, almost. In fact, the way those barges rub up against each other, they sound a bit like cows mooing. Means the cables are loose, and I see I've got some tightening to do. You always got to be thinking of what's twelve miles up ahead. Sure don't want to get caught meeting a big upbound tow where the channel's narrow. That could make you real nervous. I asked Smitty once how fast he figures we could stop, and he says maybe a half mile or more in this current. Could sure scrunch up the barges something awful in that half mile.

Wish you could have been here on the boat

this morning. I was sitting out on the stern in the sun, drinking my coffee, when this gull flaps down and starts circling 15 feet above me, head going every which way, looking for scraps. Some men toss up pieces of their doughnuts, you know. Well, just then Henderson cuts loose on Herman's whistle, and that whistle is sort of hysterical-sounding, see. That old sea gull slammed on its air brakes, stalled out, spun around, and took off like the United States Air Force was after him. Never saw such a turnaround in my life.

I hope there will be some mail from my family when I get to New Orleans, which will be about the same time you get this letter, if we're lucky. No more locks from here on, anyway. And I hope that all the news about your Aunt Lois is good news.

Hugs for you and David and Benjy, and a big smooch for Mom,

Dad

Jimmy was glad that he had written to his father, and was sure that the letter would be waiting for him when Bart Novak reached New Orleans. He had drawn a cartoon on his letter too, a boy with a big T on his shirt, for "Thonker," but the cartoon wasn't very funny. The boy was asleep on the mattress in the garage, and a big drop of rain, leaking through the ground above, was about to land on his head.

Rain was on Jimmy's mind a lot lately. It was about all he was thinking of, even more than the magic show. As he was putting on his good shoes and pants, the rain streamed in torrents down the window.

The show was to start at two o'clock, so Marsha came over at one.

"I want to call George at New Orleans and let him say 'Happy Birthday' to Kevin," Marsha told Mother. "I've never tried calling the boat before. When would be the best time, do you think?"

Jimmy knew that it had to be a special occasion to call the boat. It was expensive, and you had to call the long distance operator and ask to be connected to the marine operator of the city closest to where you figured the boat was. It had to be a big enough city to have a marine operator or at least a tower.

"If I were you, I'd try at a shift change," Mother said. "Six o'clock tonight. You can do it before we have supper, and hope that George won't mind about the cost."

"I'll tell him it's a once-in-a-lifetime thing," said Marsha, and grinned at Jimmy and David. "A baby's only one year old once in a lifetime, right?"

Jimmy grinned back, and finished the rest of his sandwich. David must have been swinging his feet back and forth under his chair because he accidentally kicked Jimmy's leg. Jimmy kicked back—lightly.

"Ow!" David whined, reaching down to rub his leg as though he had been permanently injured or something.

Jimmy kicked him again—gently. David looked as though he didn't know whether to tell on Jimmy or cry. He didn't do either one, however. He kicked back.

Good for you, Jimmy thought, and pretty soon they were kicking back and forth under the table, trying to dodge each other's feet. It was good to see David learning to take a little rough stuff.

Mother turned to Jimmy and David. "Well, guys, it's showtime! You ready to go?"

"Ready!" said David, shoving away from the table. The boys put on their jackets and raced with Mother to the car, through the pouring rain. They drove across the canal and through downtown Joliet, with its old limestone buildings, to Rialto Square.

Jimmy had only been in the Rialto Theater one other time to hear Ricky Skaggs sing Dad's favorite songs, "Waitin' for the Sun to Shine" and "Uncle Pen." David, though, hadn't been in the Rialto at all.

They entered the great hallway of mirrors and marbled columns that was supposed to look like a palace somewhere. There was a huge chandelier at the end, and water fountains with little naked angels holding them up, and bunches of gold grapes above the doorways leading into the theater itself.

"Wow!" David kept saying. "Wow!"

Mother had purchased seats in the balcony, so the boys followed her up the winding staircase, with its red carpet and the gold mermaid or something at the bottom of the banister. And finally, there they were in their seats, looking out at the glittering gold walls and the lights and the carvings in the ceiling.

"When I was a girl," Mother said, "we used to come to movies here, and I didn't think it was at all unusual for a theater to be so beautiful. I thought that *all* theaters had a stage with a big velvet curtain. It wasn't until I grew up that I realized just how special it was."

"Boy, it's special, all right!" said David, looking around. "I wish my mom could see this."

Mother just laughed. "Your mother is my *sister*, David!" she said, hugging him. "Who do you think I used to go to the movies *with*? Lois loves the Rialto, too!"

The lights dimmed at last, and Jimmy settled back to enjoy the show. The organist started to play, and slowly part of the big pipe organ rose up out of the orchestra pit on its special platform until it was even with the stage. The spotlight shone on the man who was playing show tunes. He could make the organ sound like bells or wood blocks or even violins. The audience clapped, and then the spotlight moved to the center of the curtain, and the magician himself stepped out in his black tuxedo and high silk hat. People clapped even harder. Jimmy promised himself to remember every trick the magician did so that he could tell Dad about it.

The man on stage could do almost anything, it seemed. He could rip scarves in two pieces and put them back together again. He could crawl down inside a box that hardly seemed big enough for his foot and come up a minute later with six other men behind him. Jimmy's father liked to do magic tricks, too. He could reach in somebody's ear and pull out a dime. But he couldn't do tricks like this.

When the magician called for a boy and girl from the audience to come up onstage and help, Jimmy waved his hand wildly, hoping that he would be chosen. But the magician chose a boy and girl from the rows below. The girl had on a red dress with a red ribbon holding back her ponytail, so it was easy to see how the magician chose her, but the boy just had on an ordinary shirt, like Jimmy's, and Jimmy kept thinking how it could have been him up there onstage. What a letter he could write to his dad then!

The magician had the boy and girl shake hands. Then he waved a large sheet in the air, and when he dropped it again, the girl had disappeared. The boy looked all around the stage but he couldn't find her. The magician waved the sheet once more, and the girl was standing right there again in the same spot, but without her hair ribbon. The man in the black tuxedo asked the boy to look in his pocket. The boy pulled out the girl's ribbon. The audience cheered.

"Wasn't that a good show!" Mother said when they went back down the carpeted stairway, following the crowd.

"Boy, *I* wouldn't want to be that girl who disappeared!" said David. "What if the magician couldn't bring her back?"

Jimmy laughed. "That would never happen," he said.

"I bet it could!" said David. "I saw a movie once about a magician who loved this girl and wanted her to be in a show with him and he put her in a box and sawed it in half and when he opened the box she was dead."

"Goodness!" said Mother. "You certainly watch some scary movies."

"I can remember when you used to cry at the movies," Jimmy reminded him.

"Well, I don't anymore," said David. "I just close my eyes at the scary parts."

Jimmy and Mother both laughed.

As they went back down the hall toward the entrance, Jimmy stopped thinking about the magician and thought about rain. His ears felt as though they would fall off his head because he was listening so hard for the sound of raindrops.

The crowd moved closer and closer toward the doorway and then suddenly they were outside. The rain had stopped! Jimmy wanted to shout. The air had a warm, fresh feel to it, but there was no rain at all as they walked back to the car—not even a sprinkle. It would be the perfect night for the railroad bridge. It was almost five o'clock already. Only two and a half more hours till bridge time!

15

THE BRIDGE

At six o'clock, before Kevin's birthday party began, Marsha Evans put in a phone call to the marine operator in New Orleans.

She gave the operator the boat's name, the *Herman C.*, then sat down on a kitchen stool to wait.

"How long does it usually take to reach the boat?" she asked Mother.

"Not too long if the boat's near New Orleans. If it's not, then you've got to try the marine operators at other cities up the river until you find one within radio distance of the boat."

Jimmy helped his mother set the table while she boiled the spaghetti.

"The *Herman C.*," Marsha said again, a little louder, into the telephone receiver. "It was due in today,

I think. . . ." She waited some more. "It sounds like a bad connection," she told Mother. "So much static. . . ." And finally she was talking to the marine operator again. When she hung up, she said, "Darn! The boat hasn't even gotten there yet! The operator said that they're having storms down there and to call again in a couple of hours. Do you think I should try calling upriver?"

"I don't know," said Mother, and Jimmy knew that she was worrying again. She always worried until Dad was home safe. "If they're not in New Orleans, they must be awfully close. Why don't you try again at eight? Kevin will still be awake then."

"Okay," said Marsha disappointedly, but then she brightened. "Oh, well. On with the party!"

All through the birthday supper, Jimmy's eyes were on the clock, waiting for seven-thirty. At six-twenty, Mother put the spaghetti on the table, and everyone laughed as Kevin and Benjamin tried to pick up long strands of the stuff and put it in their mouths. Marsha took a picture.

Six-forty-five: Mother brought out the cake with a clown's face in red and yellow frosting on top, with a big red candle for its nose. Marsha and David and Mother sang "Happy Birthday," while Jimmy, who couldn't carry a tune, sort of mumbled along. Then Marsha blew out the candle, set the cake in front of Kevin, and Kevin plopped both hands in the frosting. This time Mother took a picture.

Five after seven: Mother spooned ice cream into

Kevin and Benjamin while Marsha brought in the big stuffed clown that she and Mother had made. Finally, when the two babies were put in the playpen together, Jimmy knew that the party was over. He went to his bedroom to change clothes.

Now he began to feel excited. Dark Thonker T-shirt, dark jeans, his best dark Converse sneakers, navy blue jacket. . . .

"Mom," he said, coming back into the kitchen, "could we use the Monopoly set tonight? We want to play a game."

"You and David?" Mother asked.

"The *Thonkers,* Mom! It's our last night out in the garage."

"Oh. Well, I don't see why you can't invite David just to play Monopoly, Jimmy," Mother said.

Jimmy felt his chest tighten. He hadn't counted on this. What reason *could* he give for not letting David play? He was surprised when he heard David say, "It's okay. I'll just stay here and watch TV."

Jimmy couldn't believe it. "I'll play Monopoly with you tomorrow," he promised. And then, to his mother, "I'm going to take some Cokes down, too, Mom, okay? Then we'll have everything we need until morning." He got the Cokes from the kitchen and the game from the closet. "Good night, everybody," he said, trying to make it sound official. "Good night, Marsha. Happy birthday, Kevin."

"Good night, Jimmy," Marsha said. "Thanks for helping celebrate Kevin's birthday."

Heart thumping, Jimmy ran down the backyard and climbed over the fence. Peter and Sam were already there with their bikes, both dressed in dark browns and blues.

"Okay, now, listen," Jimmy said. "We've got to leave the light on and the radio playing. And we'd better spread the game out and divide up the money so it will look like we've been playing, if anyone comes in."

"Yeah. They'll think we've just walked up to my house for a minute," said Peter. He put the Monopoly pieces on the board and even a few houses on Park Place.

"I think we should leave a half can of Coke sitting here, too," Sam suggested.

So Jimmy opened a can, they took a drink, then put it there on the table beside the Monopoly game and the transistor radio. Jimmy wheeled his bike out of the garage, and they were off—Jimmy in the lead, Sam next, Peter in the rear.

It was dusk—the evening they had been talking about for a long, long time. Riding down Hickory Street, they crossed Granite, then Ruby, then Marble Street, and when they came to Lime, they turned left and went on down to Bluff. Past Stone Street they went, then Bridge Street, and still on until they came to the weeds and brush beside the ink-black water.

The bridge was huge and dark against the gray sky. In the daytime, they could see every beam on it, every plank and even the bolts on the side supports.

But now, as evening settled down around them, the railroad bridge looked like a phantom rising up out of the mist.

The boys hid their bikes in the brush and crept forward, out of sight of the bridge tender on the other side. They watched a towboat come down from Lockport and go right under the bridge. Some boats had telescoping pilothouses that could be lowered when the boat approached a bridge, but unless the railroad bridge was down, any boat could go underneath it without lowering the pilothouse.

It wasn't raining, but it was cold by the canal. The window of the bridge tender's house cast a square of yellow light on the water. It looked warm and snug in the little room where the man watched for train signals.

Jimmy kept his hands in his pockets and almost wished that he had worn gloves, even though Thonkers never wore gloves until it was cold enough to throw snowballs. It wasn't just the air that made him cold, however; it was what they were about to do. Now that they were here, Jimmy thought of all the reasons they shouldn't be. Maybe a train wouldn't come through, he thought. Maybe they could just go on home and say that if one *had* come by, they would have gone up on the bridge for sure.

A half hour went by, and then there was a screeching, grinding sound of metal against metal as the overhead span began to lower. Jimmy's heart pounded.

"A train's on the way!" said Peter.

The bridge came on down until at last the span was in place, the tracks connected, the roadbed ready.

More time went by, and the boys jumped up and down to stay warm. Jimmy's heart was jumping up and down, too. As far as he knew, no third grader had ever jumped off the railroad bridge before. Not even a fourth grader. Jimmy swallowed and tried to think. Maybe not even a *fifth* grader! There was a lot of talk about what boys were *going* to do, but the only boy whom Jimmy knew of for *sure* who had jumped was a tall boy in the sixth grade.

The minutes ticked on. Five, then ten, then fifteen. Maybe he should just tell the guys he'd changed his mind. Maybe he should say they'd go another night and then just sort of forget about it. Every time he thought of how to say it, though, he knew what the boys at school would say. *Yeah, you just chickened out.* That's what they'd say.

Suddenly Sam said, "Hey! I feel the tracks vibrating."

"It's coming!" said Peter. "I see the light."

Now, thought Jimmy as the headlight of the train grew larger. *Tell them now that we're not going to do it!* What if Peter fell in and drowned? What if it was Sam?

The train came closer, giving a shrill blast of its whistle.

Whoom! The engine went by, and then a long string of rackety freight cars, clanking on the tracks, each one sending a blast of air into the boys' faces. In the dark they couldn't see how long the train was. It was only after the noise had stopped that they realized the caboose had passed.

"Now!" Sam said, and the boys sprang forward, onto the end of the span.

Sam had hold of the bridge supports on one side, Peter had hold of a bar on the other, and Jimmy was standing on the railroad ties in the middle, holding onto nothing. The smell of oil and creosote from the railroad ties filled his nostrils. He could hear the fading roar of the train as it got farther and farther away, and the throb in his ears of his own pulse pounding.

There was still time. *Just open your mouth and tell them that this is dangerous and dumb,* Jimmy thought. His mouth didn't move, but the bridge did.

The platform beneath them began to rise. The screeching sound again, metal against metal.

Jimmy sucked in his breath. Sam was already leaning forward, peering over the edge. The ground beneath them fell away. Three feet . . . four feet . . . five. . . .

"We'd better jump!" said Sam, and his voice shook just a little.

"Now?" said Peter, and before anyone could answer, he jumped. Sam was next. The only reason Jimmy hadn't jumped yet was because his legs felt numb. A few seconds more and it would be too late.

"Jump, Jimmy!" he heard Peter whisper hoarsely.

He bent his knees and jumped.

16

FAR OFF
DOWN THE RIVER

Jimmy knew even before he landed that this was the farthest he'd ever jumped in his life. He tried to jump at an angle, aiming for the ground beside the tracks to avoid the metal rails directly in front of him. A moment before he hit the ground, he remembered too late that when you land, you often bounce; you roll.

His body brushed against Sam's on the way down and then he felt the sting of gravel on the palms of his hands. Losing his balance, he tumbled over sideways and rolled toward the edge of the canal. He felt one sneaker fly off his foot. Heard Peter's startled, "Look out!" and had time only to grasp hold of one of the metal rails of the track before he felt one leg go over the edge.

Jimmy clung tightly, and his body stopped rolling.

Sam had hold of one knee and Peter had hold of his shoulder. They were dragging him away from the edge.

For a moment the three of them crouched there, and Jimmy's heart beat so hard that it hurt. He could hear the pounding of it in his ears, the swishing *thud, thud, thud.*

"We *did* it!" Peter said finally. Breathlessly.

Sam's voice was a little shaky. "You waited too long, Jimmy. I'll bet you were ten feet up in the air."

Jimmy's voice was shaky, too. "I lost a shoe," he said. "I think it's in the canal."

They crawled around on their hands and knees searching for the shoe in the darkness.

"My best pair of Converse sneakers," Jimmy said.

"You want to come back tomorrow and look for it?" Sam asked.

"No," Jimmy told him. "I'm sure I heard it splash. Let's go home."

They called back and forth to each other as they rode back up Bluff Street, rehearsing what they would tell the other boys at school—how Jimmy had almost gone over the edge—and the more they talked, the more dangerous it sounded. Jimmy felt sick inside.

It *had* been dangerous, and Jimmy knew it. Dark and dangerous and just plain dumb. When they jumped, Jimmy had been too high, and they hadn't counted on the bounce or the roll. There were a lot of things they hadn't counted on, Jimmy thought, as they made the turn at the alley.

What was he going to tell his mother about his Converse sneaker? If he just said he'd lost it, she'd say, "Well, go look for it." If he said it was in the canal. . . . Well, he knew he couldn't tell her that.

"Hey!" said Sam. "The garage door's open."

They could see light from the doorway, and then they saw David waiting for them there.

The sick feeling in Jimmy's stomach turned to anger. David probably knew all along that they were going to the canal! That's why he didn't want to play Monopoly. He was waiting until they left so he could snoop around their clubhouse.

Jimmy hopped off his bike and leaned it against the wall, glaring at David. And then he noticed his face.

David stood there small and skinny in Jimmy's old jeans and the King Kong T-shirt. He wasn't even wearing a jacket. His face looked pale.

"What's the matter, David?" Jimmy asked. "Your mom?"

David shook his head.

"What happened, then?"

David swallowed. "It's your dad. . . ."

All Jimmy remembered later was that he started to run. He scaled the fence at the bottom of the backyard, clawed his way up the steep, muddy slope, and when he reached the kitchen with one shoe missing, no one even noticed. Mother and Marsha were sitting at the table staring at each other over two filled cups of coffee that had gone untouched.

"What's happened to Dad?" Jimmy panted. David crept in behind him and sat down, his eyes large and frightened.

"Now, Jimmy," Marsha said quickly, *"nothing's* happened to your dad that we know of. He's probably fine."

"What happened?" Jimmy demanded, almost shouting, and walked over to the table.

"Marsha finally got hold of the boat about a half hour ago," Mother told him. "They've had an accident."

Jimmy's legs felt wobbly. "Where's Dad?"

"We're not sure. They were south of Baton Rouge, trying to make that sharp bend in the river near St. Gabriel. Something either went wrong with the steering or the current was to blame, but they hit some barges at Stauffer Dock and the tow broke apart."

It was what Mother had not said that felt like an enormous rock in the pit of Jimmy's stomach, sinking lower and lower, pulling his chest down with it. A tow of barges didn't break apart unless the cables snapped. And Jimmy knew what could happen when the wires went.

"Where . . . where was Dad when it happened?" he asked.

This time Mother's voice shook just a little. "He was standing lookout on the lead barge, Jimmy, helping navigate the bend. That's all we know right now. George told Marsha that barges are going every which way down the river, and they'll be all night trying to round them up."

Jimmy turned helplessly to Marsha. "Didn't he say anything else about Dad?"

"They won't know any more till they find that barge." Marsha dropped both hands wearily in her lap. "Jimmy, I didn't even want you to know about this. George said not to say a word to either of you, because you'd only worry. But I knew if I didn't tell Carol, she'd imagine something worse. There's just a whole lot of confusion going on—George couldn't talk to Kevin, of course. There's wind and rain and hail, he says, and other towboats are moving out on the river now to help snag all the barges."

"Listen," Mother said. "Bart's gone around that bend a hundred times in bad weather."

"Things like this probably happen on the river all the time, and the men never tell us," Carol added. "It's just because I happened to call that we found out now. They'd never tell us otherwise."

"When are we going to *know*, Mom, if he's all right?" Jimmy asked.

"George said he'd call me again around eleven," Marsha said quickly, "and if he doesn't, I'll call him. He knows I'm at your house."

"Jimmy, come here," said Mother, and when he came over, she put one arm around him. The feel of Mother's hand on his back only made tears well up in his eyes. Jimmy wanted to stay there, wanted her arm around him, but not in front of David and Marsha. He stayed only a minute, then moved over to the back door and stared outside. He could see Sam and Peter waiting for him on the steps. When he was sure his tears had stopped, he went out.

"What happened, Jimmy?" Sam asked. "Is your dad okay?"

"We don't know. He was on the lead barge, and it broke loose going around a bend. All the barges are loose."

"Oh, gosh!" said Peter.

"Listen, I'm going to stay in here tonight—in case somebody calls."

"Sure," said Sam. "We'll close up the garage for you and go on home." Their voices were polite, quiet, like the voices Jimmy and his mother used just after Aunt Lois had been operated on.

Jimmy just swallowed and nodded his head.

He didn't trust himself to go back inside yet, wasn't quite sure that tears weren't going to spill out all over the place. He heard the radio stop playing in the garage, saw the light go out. Then there was the rattle of bikes as Sam and Peter rode home.

Jimmy sat down on the back steps. He could feel goose bumps on his arms, but he didn't feel the cold. Couldn't feel anything but fear. Somewhere, far off down the river, his dad was in trouble, and there was nothing Jimmy could do about it. Right at that moment, he was more frightened than he had ever been in his life. More frightened than he'd been at the railroad bridge, more scared, even, than he had been at the hospital for surgery on his knee.

He leaned against the railing and, even though he couldn't see it, stared steadily out into the blackness in the direction of the canal.

17

THE FIRST CALL

Jimmy knew about cables breaking—"wires," the boatmen called them. He knew a lot of things that his parents didn't know he knew. Several times he had walked into a room when Dad was telling Mother something that had happened on the river and noticed the way his father stopped talking. He had overheard little bits of conversation as he passed the kitchen sometimes, or things his father said on the telephone when he was talking to one of the other towboat men. He knew.

He knew that a steel cable, snapping, could whip around and cut a person in two, like a hatchet. He knew that's how a man named James Henshaw had died. He knew that's how Clyde Perkins lost a leg. When barges sideswiped each other or a bank, when they turned and jackknifed on a river, you didn't want to be anywhere near a snapping cable.

Once, when the boatmen got together at a Knights of Columbus picnic at Garnsey Park, after they'd played softball and eaten the sausage and sauerkraut the women had fixed, they'd told the story of how Bart Novak had heard a cable snapping once and had dived down into a load of coal there on the barge.

"Only thing that saved him, too," one of the boatmen had said, "but you should have seen his face when he come back out of that coal!" And they had all laughed and slapped the table. All but Jimmy.

It seemed to him now, as he sat alone on the back steps, that the river had become an enemy with a hundred tricks for catching a man and his boat.

Fog, for one thing. "Surface fog," his father called it, because it was worse right there above the water, right where the pilot needed to see. Currents were another. When the river was high, as the Mississippi was now, the currents were unpredictable. There was the suction, too, created by two boats passing each other, which could pull a boat into another one. And of course there were the shadows that might not be shadows at all. When you walked the length of a tow, from one barge to another, one misstep could put you in the water.

Unable to sit still any longer, Jimmy went back inside. The half-eaten birthday cake with the happy face seemed out of place now. Kevin and Benjamin had been put to bed, and there was hardly any noise in the kitchen. Marsha moved around putting things away, and Mother didn't even seem to notice when Marsha took the coffee mug out of her hand.

"Now *look* at the three of you!" Marsha scolded jokingly, frowning at David, too. "Moping around, worrying, while that barge has probably drifted over to the bank and Bart is on shore somewhere getting himself dry."

She stopped suddenly and Jimmy knew why. If the barge had drifted over to the bank, Dad would have gone right to a telephone and called the *Herman C.*, and George would have called here to say that Dad was all right. No news was not good news; it was simply no news at all.

Mother got up from the table and began taking all the clean dishes out of the dishwasher and putting them away. "Bart knows what to do when things like this happen on the river," she said to no one in particular.

What about James Henshaw and Clyde Perkins? Jimmy wanted to say. Weren't they supposed to have known what to do? When a cable snapped, there weren't any rules. It was all luck—all where you happened to be standing.

"Where's your other shoe?" Mother asked, glancing down at Jimmy's foot.

"I think I lost it," he mumbled.

"Well, I guess you'd better go look for it tomorrow," she said absently, and the way she looked at the clock, Jimmy knew she had forgotten the shoe already.

It was ten-fifteen. Forty-five minutes and they'd know something. If the men found the lead barge, maybe George would call sooner. Any minute, in fact, that phone might ring.

Jimmy knew that Mother and Marsha were thinking the same thing, the way they hung around the kitchen, finding things to do. Jimmy went out into the living room, where Kevin's large stuffed clown leaned crazily against the sofa. David sat on the couch holding two of Jimmy's Matchbox cars. He silently ran them over his legs and across the cushions, but he didn't look as though he were enjoying it much.

Jimmy went on down the hall to his bedroom and took off his one sneaker. Then he got out his children's encyclopedia and looked up Louisiana. There was a map. He put his finger on Baton Rouge. Just below it, the blue line marking the Mississippi River looked as though it had gone crazy, twisting and turning like a corkscrew. How did towboats ever get a long string of barges around that place even when the weather was good? Even when the current was normal?

He closed the book and held it between his knees to stop the shaking. Peter's father sold refrigerators at Sears, Roebuck, and Sam's dad was an accountant in an office. Why couldn't Bart Novak have chosen a job like that? Why did he have to be away so much, out on a river, where nobody ever knew for sure where he was? Why was it always Dad who was out there riding the head, checking wires, looking for trouble before it happened? This time, trouble went looking for him.

Sometimes, when the Novaks needed the money, Dad didn't even take his thirty days off when he had it coming to him. He'd stay at home a few days with the family, then make another run as a mate or deckhand for another barge line before going back to work on the *Herman C.*

The clock didn't seem to be moving at all. Jimmy went from the bedroom to the kitchen three or four times, sure that it would be eleven, but the hands seemed right where they were before. Now Mother and Marsha were cleaning out cupboards, stacking cans of soup on the table, and attacking the shelves with soapy water. David had brought a magazine out to the kitchen and stood in the doorway, silently turning the pages. Everyone was waiting. Waiting.

The phone surprised them by ringing at ten minutes of eleven. Jimmy and his mother stared at each other and then started to smile.

"George is calling early!" Marsha said. "They must have found Bart!"

She hurried to the phone and answered.

Jimmy waited. Mother waited, too, leaning against the table, holding a can of tomato soup in her hands.

Jimmy could tell that it was George Evans on the line again, but somehow Marsha didn't seem to be smiling. She was just listening.

"Yes . . . ," she said. "Yes, I know. . . . I see."

What? Jimmy wanted to yell. *Say something—say anything! Did they find Dad or not?*

"Listen, George," Marsha was saying finally, "there's no way I can keep this from Carol. Please

113

talk to her yourself. She knows the river a lot better than I do."

Jimmy watched the can of tomato soup drop down onto the table and roll slowly off the edge. No one bothered to pick it up. Mother went over to the telephone.

"He can only talk a minute," Marsha told her. "The phone lines are going to be tied up all night, and he's calling while he has the chance."

Jimmy edged closer to the phone himself.

"George, what have they found?" Mother was saying.

Jimmy could hear George Evans's voice on the other end—just a few words now and then, not whole sentences.

"Was he out on the barge alone?" Mother asked, and waited. "Can't they reach him on his walkie-talkie? . . . I see. . . . Yes, I know that bend in the river. It turns again at White Castle. Bart's told me about it before. . . ."

Jimmy tugged at her arm. "Radar, Mom! Can't they pick up the barge on radar?"

"What about radar, George?" Mother asked the question. Jimmy, holding onto her arm, felt the muscles slack. "I see," she said again. And finally, "Yes, *please,* George! Any word at all." She hung up and slipped one arm around Jimmy's shoulder, but she turned and faced Marsha.

"They think they've found all the barges except one, and that's the one Bart's on. They can't reach him on his walkie-talkie, but he's probably out of range."

"What about radar, Mom?" Jimmy asked again.

"They can't seem to pick the barge up on radar either. It might just be the rain. A heavy rain can blank out radar. Bart always said that."

It seemed to Jimmy that all the strength he'd had before was slipping out of the soles of his feet, and that his bones were dissolving. He slid into a chair at the table. David sat down silently beside him.

Mother seemed to know what Jimmy was thinking. "A barge simply can't sink that fast. It's got to be around somewhere."

She was wrong, Jimmy thought. If the lead barge had struck Stauffer Dock hard enough and sprung a leak, it could go down fast. He'd heard boatmen talk.

"What about rescue boats?" he said hoarsely. "What about helicopters?"

"Honey, the minute the storm stops, they'll be looking at every inch of that river," Marsha said. "You can't send boats out or helicopters up in weather like they're having. George says it's like a hurricane, almost."

Everything Marsha said seemed to make it worse. What chance did a man have standing out on the end of a breakaway barge in a hurricane?

Jimmy got up and went down the hall to his room. He lay down on his bed and tried not to think about what he was afraid had happened.

18

THE LONG NIGHT

The bed springs squeaked as David came in and sat down on the trundle bed. Jimmy turned over, his face to the wall. He didn't want to talk to David. To anybody. He just wanted to be alone. David seemed to know, because he quietly undressed and crawled under the covers.

A whole night! How would he be able to stand it? Jimmy wondered. He went over everything Mother had said, everything Marsha had said, looking for any little bit of encouragement, but none of it helped.

Surely it was midnight by now, Jimmy thought. He turned over again and looked at the clock. The hands gleamed cold white from the dresser: only eleven-thirty-three. Jimmy lay helplessly on his back, his body tense. He could hear David's gentle sleep-breathing.

For a long time Jimmy tried to think about other

things. He went over every day of spring vacation, and tried to remember what he and Sam and Peter had done in the garage so that he could tell Dad about it. He got up and went down the hall for a drink. When he came back, he recited the names of all the boys in his class at school. Then all the girls. He recited the names of all the teachers he had ever had, and all the priests at church.

Around midnight, he went back down the hall. Mother and Marsha were in the living room now. They had the TV turned on low, but neither of them seemed to be watching. Jimmy sat down on the arm of his mother's chair. She rested one hand on his knee but didn't say anything.

Marsha glanced over, however. "There's probably not going to be any news till daylight, Jimmy. At the first crack of dawn, they'll have boats out there looking for your dad. The minute we hear anything, we'll let you know."

"Even if I'm asleep?" Jimmy asked.

"We'll wake you," said Mother.

"Promise?"

She patted his knee. "Promise. Go back to bed, now."

Jimmy went into his room. He took off his jeans this time and pulled on his pajama bottoms, then crawled beneath the covers. It seemed hours and hours before the light went out in the living room and the rest of the house grew quiet. He knew that Marsha and Mother had gone to bed. More hours seemed to pass, and the longer Jimmy stayed in bed the more restless he became. He looked at the clock again. It was only two-thirty. Hours and hours hadn't gone by at all. Somehow the quiet of the house did not help make him sleepy; it made him lonely. Without the familiar comforting sounds in the other room, the worries in Jimmy's head grew bigger.

Dad could be in danger right this very minute. He could be in the water. His body could be wedged between two barges. He could have fallen in the river and been chewed up by the "wheel," as the men called the boat's propeller.

Jimmy moaned out loud and rolled over, jerking the covers. And then he realized that David was sitting up.

Jimmy lay still.

"Jimmy?" David whispered. "Are you awake?"

At first Jimmy wasn't going to answer. But even talking to David seemed better than spending the rest of the night by himself. "Yeah," he said finally.

"I know how you feel," David said. "The worst thing is not being there."

That was it exactly.

"Yeah," Jimmy said again. "If I was there with Dad, even if it was scary, I could try to do something. I'd at least know what was going on. It's awful to think that right now he could be. . . ." Jimmy couldn't finish. His voice choked up and he realized that he was crying.

For a few moments he cried silently, breathing through his mouth so that David couldn't hear.

"That's just how I felt," David said. "About Mom."

It was such a relief to talk to someone—anyone—

that Jimmy didn't really care if David knew he was crying or not. That just wasn't important now.

"H . . . how did you get through it?" he asked, his nose clogged. It was a dumb question, he knew, because you didn't have much choice. The minutes and hours ticked by whether you were ready for them or not.

"I just thought about the good things," David said.

"What good things?"

"Like how Mom wasn't supposed to lift heavy things, but when I sprained my ankle, she carried me inside the house. I figured maybe she was stronger than the doctors thought. Things like that."

Jimmy thought about his father working on the boat in his leather vest with the goatskin lining that Mother had given him one Christmas—the cartoon man with the cowhide gloves. The other men might be wearing heavy jackets, but half the time Dad just got by with his gloves, that vest, and his life jacket on top of it. Cold never seemed to bother him much. That's how tough he was.

But what if, when the cable snapped, Dad had been thrown into the water? The water was still cold in April, especially where it was deep, and the lower part of the Mississippi River was the deepest of all. You couldn't stay in the water very long without freezing to death. Sometimes the cold was so numbing you couldn't begin to swim.

David seemed almost to know what Jimmy was thinking.

"Remember that time Mom and I came to visit

you and we all went swimming at Braidwood and the water was so cold we couldn't go in?" he said. "Your dad did, though. He just dived in and swam right out to the raft. Remember?"

Jimmy did remember. His dad was in good shape. He didn't have a big potbelly like some men did when they worked the boats, eating all that good food. If anybody could survive the wind and the cold, it was Bart Novak.

For a while the room was quiet. Then David said, "There's a game Mom and I play sometimes. When she's going to give me something nice, she'll say, 'David, how would you like a million dollars?' And I know she doesn't have a million dollars, so I'll say, 'No, thanks.' Then Mom will say, 'How would you like a new Cadillac?' I know we can't afford a Cadillac either, so I'll say, 'Huh-uh.' And finally she'll say, 'How would you like to go to the circus?' And I'll say, 'Sure!' "

Jimmy found himself smiling just a little. "How does that help?"

"Well, when she went in the hospital for her operation I'd play that game with myself. 'Hey, David, how would you like a trip to Hawaii?' 'No, thanks,' I'd say. 'How would you like a new house with a swimming pool?' 'Nope.' 'How would you like your mom to get well?' 'Sure!' I'd say."

Jimmy silently tried it out. *Hey, Jimmy, how would you like a Yamaha motorcycle? Naw. A ten-speed bike? Nope. How would it be if they found your dad and he was okay?* "I'd like that just fine," Jimmy whispered to himself.

He imagined David playing that game alone on his way to school in a new town where the kids called him "Sissy Pants." Imagined David playing it while he ate his Rice Chex in the morning, while he watched TV—all the times when Jimmy had wondered whether David was thinking about his mother or not. He was thinking about her, all right.

When he looked over at David again, all he saw was a hump under the covers of the trundle bed. The hands of the clock read three in the morning, and David had gone back to sleep. Maybe now he could sleep, too.

Jimmy turned over and pulled the covers up tightly under his chin. But the "what ifs" would not leave him alone. What if he never saw his dad again? What if the last memory he'd ever have of him was of Dad jumping back on the barge that day at the Brandon Road lock, just after David had come?

And then, like ice water rushing down his throat, Jimmy realized that since his father had not reached New Orleans, he had not got Jimmy's letter. The last memory Dad would have of *him* would be the way Jimmy had sulked there at the Brandon Road lock when Dad had said he'd take David fishing on the Kankakee. Jimmy hadn't even said good-bye when Dad walked back to the barge, hadn't even waved.

He turned over on his stomach and pressed his face hard against the pillow.

19

THE SECOND CALL

It was only four in the morning when Jimmy woke up again and he knew he would not go back to sleep. He sat up on one elbow and looked out the window at the sky. Nothing but blackness. No moon. No stars. Then he propped his pillow against the wall and sat there watching for the first faint signs of dawn.

He tried to imagine what was happening on the *Herman C.* Usually the pilot and the captain took turns steering while the other slept, but no one would have gone to bed last night. George Evans certainly wouldn't. Dad's best friend would stay awake as long as it took to find Jimmy's father.

Jimmy knew about the flares and rockets a boatman was supposed to use as distress signals. He'd looked at his dad's manual. A boatman should also, the manual said, sound his horn, ring his bell, or fire off his gun at short intervals.

The problem was that even if Bart Novak was still safe somewhere on that barge, he wouldn't have any flares, rockets, horns, bells, or guns. Wherever he was, he had to wait until daylight. So did Jimmy.

The springs on the trundle bed squeaked as David turned in his sleep, and then his breathing came easily again, with little popping sounds at the end of each breath.

In a few hours, Jimmy thought, he would know what had happened to Dad. David, however, had gone days without knowing whether his mother would be all right. First the heart operation, then the hours that Aunt Lois had spent in the recovery room, then the days she had spent in intensive care. . . . He wondered if he himself would have been brave enough to get on a plane alone and fly to another city, not knowing what was happening to his mother back home. How did David stand it? It must have been the most difficult thing he had ever done.

Four o'clock became five, and the first streaks of pink appeared in the sky. When five became six, Jimmy could just make out the shadowy forms of trees beyond the window. He knew that on the *Herman C.*, the forward watch, from six in the morning to noon, had begun.

If this was just a normal day on the river, the pilot, the second engineer, and the deckhands would be going to bed and the captain, the first engineer, and the first mate would take over. But this was not a normal day. The first mate was missing.

Jimmy heard soft noises in the kitchen, so he got up and went down the hall. Marsha was asleep on the sofa, but Mother was in the kitchen starting a new pot of coffee. Jimmy could tell by her eyes that she had not slept very much. Probably not at all.

"We'll be going to early Mass," she said when she saw him there in the doorway. "When you dress, put on your Sunday clothes."

Jimmy sat down at the table, miserable. He didn't want to go to church. It was important, he knew, especially now, but he would rather stay right here by the telephone until he knew his dad was all right. *If* Dad was all right. . . .

He took the glass of orange juice his mother handed him and sat turning it around and around on the table. All the fun things he had done with his dad came flooding back. He was remembering last summer when Joliet celebrated its "Waterway Daze." The American Legion Band gave a concert while Jimmy's family had a picnic on the grass. Then there was Mass, and the Blessing of the Boats, and after that, dancing to the music of Frankie Yankovic, "The Polka King." What would a day like that be without Dad?

"Wear your blue pants," Mother was saying, "your gray sweater, and your best shoes."

She was trying to pretend that things would be all right, trying to show Jimmy that things would go on just as they had before, no matter what. He had to tell her. . . .

"I'll have to wear my old shoes," he said. "I lost one of my Converse sneakers." He wondered if she would remember his telling her that the night before.

This time her voice was sharp. "How can you just lose a shoe, Jimmy? Keep looking until you find it."

Jimmy stared down at the table. "I . . . I think it's in the canal, Mom." He couldn't lie to her. Not today.

She whirled around and stared down at him, waiting.

"I know we shouldn't have been there," Jimmy said.

"Last night? You and Peter and Sam?"

He nodded. "I'm sorry."

"What were you doing there?" Now her voice was loud. The words seemed to have edges on them, and cut as they came at him from across the table.

"It was dumb," Jimmy said, and there was scarcely any breath to his voice. He took a big gulp of air. "We rode the railroad bridge up a little way and jumped off. My shoe fell into the canal."

Even though he wasn't looking at her directly— he *couldn't*—he saw her body stiffen, saw her fingers grip the edge of the chair more tightly, the knuckles white.

"Jimmy Novak!" Now she was shouting. Jimmy was startled. He saw Marsha sit up on the couch. "Last night . . . ," Mother's voice was shaking now, ". . . while your father . . ." She stopped, and Jimmy was sure she would lower her voice, but she went right on shouting. "Do you know what could have *happened* to you? Do you know how I would have felt?"

Jimmy glanced up at her. Mother looked very

strange. Her mouth was all twisted, and suddenly her eyes scrunched up and tears poured down her cheeks. She sat down on the chair, hands over her face.

Marsha was in the kitchen now, her hair all mussed up, her voice hoarse with sleep. She had her hands on Mother's shoulders.

"Carol, let me make you some breakfast," she said. Already the shouting had wakened one of the babies. There were noises now from Mother's room.

Jimmy left his orange juice on the table and fled to the back bedroom. How *could* he have done something so stupid as jump off that bridge? How *could* he have taken such a chance? Numbly, he got his Sunday clothes from the closet and dressed. David slept through it all.

When he went back in the kitchen, Mother was still sitting at the table, and Marsha was making French toast.

Marsha didn't play around. "Jimmy," she said right off, placing a fat piece of French toast on his plate and then plunking the syrup bottle down beside it, "You know what 'brave' means?" And then she answered for him: " 'Brave' is when you do something dangerous and scary because somebody *has* to do it."

Jimmy nodded. Dad was out on the lead barge last night helping the pilot because someone had to do it, but there was no reason in the world why Jimmy had to be on that railroad bridge.

Mother was all through shouting now. "You figure out a way to earn the money for a new pair of sneakers," she said to Jimmy, "and never, ever, go near that bridge again."

Jimmy nodded a second time. At least she was giving him a chance to make up for it. Giving him a job he could do. For a moment he almost felt better, and then he remembered his dad. If only he could "earn" his dad home again. He swallowed his bite of toast without tasting.

Kevin woke up and added his fussing to Benjamin's, and soon the kitchen was noisy with everyday sounds—cereal bowls clinking, high chairs squeaking, the grunts and squeals of the babies. It must be nice to be so young that you didn't understand anything, Jimmy thought. Benjy didn't even know that Dad was gone. Didn't even miss him.

It was seven-twenty-nine when the call came. David had just gotten up, Marsha had taken Kevin into Mom's bedroom to change him, Mother was wiping Benjy's face with a cloth, and Jimmy was putting silverware in the dishwasher. The phone rang, and it was like an alarm going off. They all stopped what they were doing and stared at it, and then Mother, her face drawn, lifted the receiver.

"Hello?" she said loudly, impatiently, as though whoever was calling should have called sooner. And then Jimmy saw her lift one hand to her throat, saw her eyes close, saw her reach blindly for a chair and sit down.

"Oh, Bart!" she said. "You don't know how wonderful it is to hear your voice."

20

A THONKER AT LAST

It's *Dad!*" Jimmy screamed, standing up so quickly that his chair tipped over backward. And then everyone cheered, including Marsha, who had come running out of the bedroom, and Mother's face broke into a huge smile, even though she was crying at the same time.

Mother hardly talked at all, just sat there saying, "Oh, Bart . . ." Jimmy hung onto her arm, trying to hear, until at last it was his turn on the telephone.

"Dad!" he said, and Mother let him have her place in the chair.

"Hey, Buddy!" came the cartoon man's voice.

"Are you okay?"

"I'm okay," Dad said. "But I wouldn't want to spend another night like that, I can tell you."

"What happened?"

128

"Well, when that barge cut loose, I lost my walkie-talkie in the water, trying to duck the lines. I guess the barge got caught in the slack current along shore, 'cause it carried me right down river to that towhead this side of Point Clair. Got stuck right there on the island. All the other barges went downriver in the mainstream, the other side of the towhead, and there I am for the night in the middle of that storm."

"Why couldn't they pick you up on radar?" Jimmy asked.

" 'Cause the island was in the way. Got the island there on their screen, big as life, but radar won't tell you what's on it."

"What did you *do*, Dad?" Jimmy asked. "Weren't you freezing?"

He loved the sound of his father's laughter over the phone. "I was cold, let me tell you, but that barge was carrying about a thousand tons of shelled corn. So I just opened the cover, crawled down inside, and let that corn close around me like a blanket. Only thing I got to worry about, I told myself, is I'm not eaten to death by pigeons."

Jimmy and his dad both laughed. Wait till the other guys heard that!

"We were *worried*, Dad," Jimmy said finally.

"Well, it's okay to worry some. I did my share of worrying, too, you can bet. When I saw the *Herman C.* coming back upriver to look for me, and then George coming for me in the yawl, I sang out, let me tell you, and you know how I sound when I sing!"

They laughed some more.

"So right now I'm back on board, ready to take a hot shower, but I knew you folks would be worried. You save me a piece of Kevin's birthday cake now, you hear?"

"I'll cut you the biggest piece," Jimmy promised. "And, Dad, you've got a letter from me waiting for you in New Orleans. I'm going to start another letter, too, about the magic show."

"Then I've got *two* things to look forward to," Dad said.

Such laughter and talk and celebrating when Jimmy hung up the phone! Mother hugged everyone there in the kitchen, and when she hugged Jimmy, her arms felt just as warm and soft as they always had. Jimmy called Sam and Peter.

Marsha took care of the babies while the others went to Mass, and after church, even before they had lunch, Mother drove Jimmy and David to Baskin Robbins and the three of them sat around laughing and eating ice cream. Laughed at everything and laughed at nothing. Just because it felt so good.

The Thonkers were meeting that afternoon, so when Jimmy finished the comics, he went into the bedroom to change clothes. David was putting on the King Kong T-shirt that he'd worn every day.

Jimmy watched him tying his sneakers, looked at his skinny little arms sticking out beneath the sleeves of the shirt, his knobby knees poking through the jeans.

"Hey, David," Jimmy said. "How would you like to have your own gym with weight-lifting equipment and an indoor track?"

David looked up at him and laughed. "No, thanks."

"No?" said Jimmy. "How would you like to have your own yacht, then, with a ship-to-shore radio and color TV?"

"Nope," said David, and giggled.

"Well, how would you like to come out to our club-house today, then?"

David stopped giggling and stared. "You *mean* it?" he said.

"I mean it," said Jimmy.

David grinned shyly, like he was trying to hold it back, but the smile just crept out anyway. He got up and followed Jimmy down the hall, through the kitchen, and out the back door.

Peter and Sam were already in the garage, wearing their Thonker T-shirts and sharing a bag of potato chips. When they saw David, they glanced at each other and rolled their eyes. Then they remembered Jimmy's father.

"It's sure good news about your dad, Jimmy," Sam said. "I know you were worried."

Jimmy sat down beside them. "You want to know something? That was the worst thing I ever went through in my life."

Peter stopped chewing. "No kidding?" he said. "Even scarier than jumping off the you-know-what?"

"Scarier than that. You know something else? That

wasn't even brave. It was just plain stupid." And he repeated what Marsha had said: "Brave is when you do something dangerous and scary because somebody *has* to do it."

"What about that night last year when we were fooling around in St. John's Cemetery?" Sam reminded him. "Remember when some guy came by on his bike and told us that a couple of convicts had escaped from Stateville and they were supposed to be armed and dangerous? And we had to make it all the way home in the dark?"

"I'll go through that any time before I go through last night," Jimmy said.

Peter stared. "What about your operation?" he croaked.

"It still wasn't as bad as worrying about somebody else and not being there to help. Isn't that right, David?"

"Yeah," David agreed.

"That's why we've got a new Thonker," Jimmy said, and now Sam stopped chewing, too. David was staring.

"Him?" said Sam.

Jimmy nodded.

"Hey, listen, we're supposed to decide together on new members," said Peter. "You can't do it alone, even if you *are* the Number One Thonker."

"Okay," said Jimmy. "How long were you scared when you and your mom almost went into the river in her car?"

"You know, Jimmy. A few minutes or so."

"And how long were you scared, Sam, when you broke your arm?"

"We already decided that," Sam said. "A few hours, I guess."

"Well, David had to fly out here to Joliet alone and worry about his mom for days. I only had to worry about my dad for one night, and I wouldn't want to go through that again in a million, billion years. So I say that until David goes back to Cincinnati in two weeks, we make him an honorary Thonker, and he gets to go anywhere we do. All in favor?"

There was a long silence in the garage.

"He hasn't got a T-shirt," said Sam.

"I'll get one for him," Jimmy said.

"He hasn't got a bike," Peter protested.

"He can ride on mine," said Jimmy.

"He never got a staple in his thumb or pins in his hand and he never ate a bug," said Sam.

"Big deal," Jimmy told them.

Sam sighed. "All right," he said at last. "He can be an honorary member then."

"For two weeks," said Peter.

"Besides," said Jimmy, "you haven't heard scary stories until you've heard *David's* stories!"

Sam and Peter looked at David. David was looking at Jimmy.

"Remember that last one you told me?" Jimmy said.

David scrunched up his forehead. "Which one?"

he asked. "The one about this huge spider that gets down inside the boy's sneaker and when he puts in his foot it bites him and then his toe falls off and the poison goes up into his leg and . . . ?"

"Not that one," said Jimmy.

"The one about the murderer who was a pizza delivery man and every time he came to a house he smothered the person with the pizza and . . . ?"

"No. Remember the storm the other day and you said. . . ."

"Oh. The one where lightning came in over the wires and out of the electric socket and set the boy's bed on fire."

"Yeah. That one," said Jimmy. "Tonight it will be your turn to tell a story."

"There's school tomorrow. We have to sleep at home tonight," Sam reminded him.

"You'll *want* to sleep at home when you've heard David," said Jimmy. "Come on. Let's ride over to Garnsey Park and look around." He picked up his bike and wheeled it out to the alley. David followed.

"Did you ever ride on handlebars, Killer?" Jimmy asked him.

David shook his head.

"Well, you're a Thonker now. Think you can do it?"

David took a deep breath. "Sure," he said, and shakily climbed up on Jimmy's handlebars, holding on for dear life.

"You guys coming?" Jimmy asked Sam and Peter,

who were still staring at him from the garage, "or you want to be left behind?"

"We're coming," said Sam, and got up quickly.

They rode in formation down the alley toward Garnsey Park, Peter in the rear, Sam next, Jimmy in the lead, and David on the handlebars, right at the very front of the line.